Janie could hear the slow, plodding footsteps and the loud, raspy breathing of the monstrous man who was pursuing her. She yanked open a sink drawer – pulled out a long, sharp butcher's knife.

The back door crashed in on her in a shower of splinters. He didn't seem to see the knife that she held – or else he didn't care. With all her remaining strength, she swung the butcher's knife in an upwards arc and heard his breath as the blade punctured his soft flesh. His vacant, mindless gaze never wavered, as with a sick roar he dropped her and she scrambled to her feet.

Then she watched, astounded, as he pulled the long knife out of his stomach and dropped it as if he had removed a splinter . . .

By the same author

The Awakening
Black Cat
Bloodsisters
Day Care
Limb to Limb
Majorettes
Midnight
Night of the Living Dead

JOHN RUSSO

Inhuman

GRAFTON BOOKS

A Division of the Collins Publishing Group

LONDON GLASGOW
TORONTO SYDNEY AUCKLAND

Grafton Books
A Division of the Collins Publishing Group
8 Grafton Street, London W1X 3LA

A Grafton UK Paperback Original 1987

Copyright © John Russo 1986

ISBN 0-586-07314-0

Printed and bound in Great Britain by
Collins, Glasgow

Set in Times

Mankind is poised midway between
the gods and the beasts
— PLOTINUS

I've been grappling with an old reptile
at the top of my spine
— DAVID BOTTOMS

1

'Snakes are a-comin' . . . great big snakes . . . a-comin'
to kill us,' Mary Monohan babbled.

Her daughter Sarah, on her way into Mary's bedroom
to spoonfeed her some grits and black-eyed peas, froze in
the doorway, half expecting the bedridden old lady to
start quoting scripture. But she didn't this time. She
didn't say a word about Mark, chapter sixteen, verse
eighteen: *They shall take up serpents; and if they drink
any deadly thing, it shall not hurt them; they shall lay
hands on the sick, and they shall recover.*

At age seventy-three, Mary Monohan had been an
invalid for the past six years, ever since the day she
walked into the old tarpaper shanty and a six-foot-long
blacksnake dropped on her head, draping its heavy coils
around her neck before it fell from the rafters to the floor
and slithered through a crack in the boards. Sarah, out
working in the garden – Mary had gone to fetch a hoe –
came running soon as she heard the hysterical screams.
She knew that little six-year-old Janie was with her
grandma and feared that something awful had happened
to the child. By the time Sarah got to the shanty,
Mary wasn't screaming anymore. Janie stumbled out,
whitefaced and shaky. Then Mary came out with the hoe
in her hand, but she moved like a zombie and her eyes
were glazed and empty.

Sarah took the hoe and asked what on earth had
happened, eyeing her mother and daughter for signs of
injury, but Mary's mouth was clamped shut. Janie
blurted, 'A big black snake . . . fell on Grandma . . .
ugly . . . *ugly!*' Mary didn't talk the rest of that day, even

7

during supper. That night she took to her room and didn't leave it anymore. Sarah had to wait on her hand and foot from that day on, feeding her, giving her sponge baths, and even helping her to use the chamber pot.

Sarah's husband, George Stone, wanted to put Mary into Mayview Hospital in nearby Carsonville. But Sarah swore she'd never commit her own mother to the crazy house, not as long as the good Lord gave her the strength to do her Christian duty.

They shall take up serpents; and if they drink any deadly thing it shall not hurt them . . .

Sarah's daddy, Reverend Brady Monohan, had quoted Mark 16:18 many times. He had preached it, believed in it, and used it to prove that a righteous, God-fearing man could subdue the forces of evil. Bitten by a deadly timber rattler coiled around his bare arm, he had died in front of his own congregation, praising the Lord Jesus Christ. He disdained the desperate, sobbing pleas of his young wife Mary, who wanted to slash the fang marks with a sharp knife and suck out the poisoned blood. Sarah was there too, eight years old at the time, crying and praying and watching her daddy's arm and head swell up and turn bluish black. Five hours later, he was dead.

Mama always said that it was Satan who had killed Daddy – Satan in the guise of a serpent. All her life she had been deathly afraid of snakes. After Daddy died, her fear reached horrendous proportions. If she happened to spy a small garter snake in the woods or near the garden, it would shake her up for the rest of the day – but she always eventually came out of it. Till the blacksnake fell on her in the shanty. It was like she had come face to face with the devil and her soul had withered inside her.

Now, six years after the blacksnake incident, Sarah was stunned when Mary opened her mouth to say 'snakes are a-comin'.' It was seldom that Mary ever showed that she still had the use of her tongue. Every time she *had* spoken – maybe ten times in the past six years – it had been to predict some dire, awful thing – and about half of the predictions had miraculously come true. For instance, one time she had said that Sarah's stepbrother Tom was going to be found dead in his kitchen, and sure enough the very next morning that was where he keeled over and died of a heart attack.

Sarah believed that her mother had gotten a gift of the Holy Spirit to take the place of the normal, everyday faculties of speech and movement that had been stolen from her by the blacksnake in the shanty. God in His mysterious way had compensated her for what she had lost. That was why Mary could sometimes see into the future, as could the saints and prophets of the Old Testament.

The old woman refused to eat any grits and black-eyed peas, no matter how many times Sarah put the spoon up to her lips. She kept pressing her mouth tightly shut and turning her head away. It was all Sarah could do to make her take a few sips of hot sassafras tea. 'Please eat somethin', Mama,' Sarah pleaded. 'You'll never get better if'n you don't keep your strength up.'

'Great big snakes a-comin' to *kill* us!' Mary said, her sunken eyes gleaming with the holy gift of prophecy.

Sarah shuddered, remembering her brother-in-law Tom dead in his own kitchen, when all the folks round about could swear he was a big, strapping, robust man, hardly sick a day in his life, always out ploughing his fields or mending his fences, come rain or come shine. Yet, Mary had turned out to be right about him. She had foretold that he would be struck down. God had given her the power to know things that normal people couldn't know.

What if she were speaking the Lord's truth *this* time?

She sounded so convincing, so solemn and wise, even though her actual words didn't seem to make much sense.

9

'Snakes are a-comin'. Great big snakes a-comin' to kill us.'

Sarah shuddered when she thought of the huge, poisonous vipers slithering out of the woods to attack her and her family.

2

A few minutes before they were told of Mary Monohan's prediction, Drs Charles and Anita Walsh were relaxing on the wide flagstone veranda of Carson Manor, a ten-bedroom brick mansion with gracefully slender white pillars and tall white-shuttered windows. They were eating a lunch served to them by their black housekeeper and cook, Brenda Meachum. Brenda and her twenty-year-old daughter Meredith were eating together in the kitchen, having declined the Walshes' invitation to sit with them at the picnic table. Charles and Anita were uncomfortable employing servants and couldn't stifle their inclination to treat them as equals; however, it was gradually dawning on them that the servants were uncomfortable with the 'equal' treatment and wished their employers would just drop it and get used to being waited on.

The Walshes were both psychiatrists with a joint practice in Richmond, on the other side of the state. Charles was forty-five, of average height, slender, but in good physical condition from playing handball three days a week back in the city despite the difficulty of scheduling his patients around his exercise sessions. His hair was thick and white, having turned prematurely grey when he was in his thirties. But his complexion was ruddy and wrinkle-free, and his blue eyes had a youthful glint of intelligence and enthusiasm.

Anita Walsh was six years younger than her husband, and would have looked ten years younger than him if she wasn't a bit plump – perhaps fifteen pounds overweight. Her long hair, tied back in a bun, was naturally black, not dyed, and in her white blouse and tan slacks she had the big breasts and voluptuous curves of a large but attractive woman. However, one of her goals this summer was to lose the excess poundage. While Charles enjoyed fried chicken, home fries, and green beans, Anita suffered through a lump of cottage cheese washed down with diet cola.

'I wish I could be like you,' she complained to her husband. 'You never gain, no matter how much you eat.'

'Because I burn off the extra calories,' said Charles. 'If I didn't, they'd turn to fat.'

'I exercise, too,' Anita defended. 'But I have a different metabolism than you do. If you had my metabolism you'd find out how miserable it is to have to diet all the time.'

'Actually there's nothing wrong with your weight,' Charles said with a lecherous wink. 'I like you the way you are – amply endowed. The Victorian ideal. The perfect mistress of Carson Manor.'

'Yes, I fit right in with all the antiques,' Anita said, feigning a whimper, pretending not to be pleased by her husband's compliment. But she smiled as she sipped her diet cola and watched him enjoying a mint julep – his way of revelling in his role as master of the plantation.

They both gazed out over the brick courtyard and the vast expanse of front lawn sheltered by sycamore and weeping willow trees. In love with Carson Manor, they still could not get over the fact that they owned it. It was a dream come true, a peaceful country retreat in the foothills of the beautiful Shenandoah Mountains. Anita's Uncle Horace, a wealthy antique dealer, had willed the property to her – but although Charles and Anita had loved it on sight, they at first had believed that they could never afford to maintain it and pay the yearly taxes. But finally they had talked themselves into keeping it, realizing that they could make it provide supplementary income and tax write-offs while they relaxed and enjoyed themselves during the summers. Their means of doing this was to hold 'marriage encounters' – matrimonial therapy sessions – at Carson Manor four days of each week, June through July. That gave them three days out of seven to be by themselves and to work on the psychiatric articles and books that they published together. August was set aside as a vacation month. The rest of the year was devoted to their practice in Richmond.

Anita got a kick out of Charles's behaviour when they were at the Manor. During their summers here, he became like the place itself – an anachronism; an antebellum gentleman sipping mint juleps and 'overseeing the plantation' in high-topped boots, jodphurs, and wide-brimmed Stetson, a colourful bandana cinched at the collar of his tight-cuffed, white, full-sleeved shirt. He had even coaxed Anita into taking riding lessons with him, and now they owned matching palomino horses, which were kept in the stable behind the house.

Charles had a powerful interest in the history of the Old South and the Confederacy, even though he was a native Northerner, born and raised in Cleveland. While he deplored the institution of slavery, he was charmed by the ideals of the patrician class that slavery had supported, and he considered those romantic ideals of honour and chivalry to be superior to the shabby cynicism of modern times. He had come to Richmond Hospital to do his internship, and that was when he had met Anita Bledsoe, while she was still an undergraduate at the University of Virginia. Perhaps because she had grown up immersed in 'Southern heritage', Anita wasn't as enamoured of it as Charles was. The few times she had visited her Uncle Horace's country estate as a child, she had found it stuffy and oppressive – crammed with old, musty stuff instead of stuff that was shiny, streamlined, and new. But now that Carson Manor belonged to her and Charles, she adored it. She had never expected her penny-pinching uncle to will it to her; it would've been more like him to donate it to the state as a museum.

'You know,' she told Charles, 'when I was a teenager I thought this place was the pits. Dull. Boring! I hated to come here with my parents to visit Uncle Horace. I wanted to be back in Richmond with my friends – caught up in a whirl of movies, dances, and parties. But now that I'm older, the mere idea of such a hectic pace appalls me. I wonder how I could've been such a frantic youth, blind to all this loveliness and serenity.'

'Youth doesn't crave serenity,' Charles said with a sardonic gleam in his eyes. 'Too much sap in the veins. Youth craves thrills, excitement, and wild, crazy sex.'

'Well, I didn't mean that I'm *completely* over the hill,' Anita chided good-naturedly. 'Once in a while I crave some of those other things, too. Don't you?'

'If Brenda had made this mint julep any stronger, I don't think I'd be craving anything but a nap,' Charles said after swallowing the watery dregs of his drink. He set the glass down, stood up and stretched, and heard the sound of tyres on gravel as George Stone's battered old pickup turned on to the driveway, bringing George and his daughter Janie back from lunch.

'They're a half hour early,' said Anita, glancing at her watch. 'I wonder why.'

'We're such nice people to work for,' said Charles. 'They can't stand to be away from us.'

'More likely they're just anxious to get away from Sarah,' Anita chuckled. 'She's always nagging them to death.'

The Walshes both waved as George and Janie Stone got out of the pickup truck and walked across the brick courtyard. A tall, rawboned, redheaded man in bibbed coveralls, plaid shirt, and scuffed-up clodhoppers, George always had a beaten, world-weary look. He had given up farming to become a coal miner and then the mines had shut down. Now he was part of the 'underground economy' – collecting welfare payments and food stamps and not bothering to report any cash he earned as caretaker of Carson Manor.

This summer, as soon as school let out, Janie started tagging along with her daddy about twice a week, to help out at the Manor and earn herself some spending money. Twelve years old now, with red hair and freckles, she resembled George – even wore tomboyish bibbed coveralls over her tee shirt – except she still had the sprightly energy and enthusiasm that had been beaten out of her daddy.

George took off his red, sweat-stained baseball cap and held it in front of him in both hands, his shoulders slumped in a submissive posture as he trudged up the steps of the veranda to confront his employers. Janie wasn't so inhibited. She skipped up the steps beside her daddy, calling out, 'Hi, Doctor Chuck! Hi, Doctor Anita!' – impervious to the sideways look George gave her for not behaving in a more 'respectful' way toward 'the gentry'.

'Have a seat, relax a while,' Charles said with cheerful camaraderie. 'We accomplished a lot this morning. No need to drive ourselves too hard this afternoon.'

'Well,' George said, giving his daughter another sideways glance, 'I already told Janie I want her to get started right away grooming Bullet and Lightning.'

'I want to do it *now!*' Janie blurted, itching to spend some time alone with the two palominos.

'Go right ahead, Miss Ants-in-the-Pants,' George told her. 'I reckon you know where the curry brush is. Don't play around with it. Do a good job. You'll know it's done right when your arm feels like it's gonna drop off. Then you can give the animals each a bag of oats.'

'Oh boy! Can I?' Janie enthused.

'Yep,' said George. 'Now hurry up and – '

15

But he was wasting his breath telling her to hurry, because she was already scampering off the veranda, her red ponytails flapping as she jumped down the last three steps and ran around the side of the house toward the stable.

Charles and Anita chuckled. But George didn't. Obviously he had something on his mind. He cleared his throat and said, 'According to Sarah, my mother-in-law's found her tongue again. Just before noon, she babbled somethin' about snakes comin' to kill us. Don't make no sense. But Sarah said Mama kept repeatin' it . . . three or four times in all.'

'Did she say anything else?' Charles asked.

'Nope. Just the thing about snakes . . . great big snakes a-comin' to kill us.' George shook his head, embarrassed about having a mother-in-law in such a condition.

'Do you want me to go over and try to get her to open up a bit more?' Charles asked.

'I'd be much obliged if'n you would,' said George.

They drove to the Stone place in Charles's Land Rover, a three-mile drive on the bumpy dirt road that wound through the fields and forests of Carson Valley. Just about everything around here was named after the Carson family who had owned it all up till the end of the Civil War. Carson Valley. Carson Manor. Carson Creek. Carson Valley Church of Christ. The nearest town, population 1,016, eighteen miles away, was called Carsonville. The estate that Charles and his wife now owned was but a small part of a once grand and flourishing plantation that had been ruled and operated like a huge medieval fiefdom. After the abolishment of slavery, the Carson family, decimated and reduced to financial ruin by the struggle to preserve the Confederacy, had been forced to sell out to a carpetbagger, who had broken the land up into small parcels worked by sharecroppers and tenants.

Today, Carson Valley was mostly unpopulated, the countryside dotted with burned-out, tumbled-down houses, barns, and shanties. Most of the fields were overgrown, unplanted. The folks who were left, like the Stones, didn't farm much anymore; instead they tried to scrape by on the meagre work available in distant mines, stores, and factories.

As he drove, Dr Charles Walsh explained to George Stone that there really wasn't much chance of getting through to Mary Monohan. 'Still, the best time to try is when she has already started to speak, of her own volition. That's when she may be most receptive to additional communication. So I'm going to give it my best shot, but I don't want to give you and Sarah any false hopes.'

'I understand, Doctor Chuck,' George said sombrely. 'And as far as my wife is concerned, she done give up on Mama, to the point where she said that there was no use of my even askin' you to come.'

They parked and jumped out of the Land Rover in front of a decrepit old farmhouse with peeling, greying white paint and rusty tin roof. The dog chained in the back yard started barking furiously. Meanwhile, Sarah came out on to the sagging front porch. Switching his black leather doctor's bag from his right hand to his left, Charles tipped his tan Stetson towards her. The psychiatrist was sensitive to the feelings hidden behind people's words, and he thought that the bony, brittle-haired, stiff-backed farmwoman didn't really like his being here, even though she made a show of thanking him for his trouble and welcoming him into her home. 'The Lord's will,' she said, nervously rubbing her big-knuckled hands on the threadbare apron that she wore over her faded print housedress. 'The Lord's will, and nothing us poor sinners can do to change it. Go on up and try to talk to Mama, but I doubt you'll get anything

17

more out of her than what I could. After all, I'm her own flesh and blood, and she trusts me more'n she trusts anybody.'

Charles wondered if perhaps Sarah didn't want her mother to get well. He had seen it before in his patients: the dread of the loss of meaning and purpose in a life that had become utterly focused on a helpless, dependent person. If the dependency suddenly ended, it could produce a profound emptiness instead of a feeling of relief and release from a crushing burden.

From the living room, full of old, worn, overstuffed furniture, George led Charles up the banistered, uncarpeted stairs, and they entered Mary Monohan's room. Charles recoiled from the stale, hot, sweaty odour. The windows were shut and the gas heater was turned on, and the June sun was beating on the tin roof, and yet the invalid was lying under several blankets, sunken into her pillow and feather tick like a person trying to be absorbed into nonexistence.

'Good afternoon, Mary,' Charles said. 'How are you feeling?' She didn't answer, but he went on talking, peeling back the blankets and sheet to examine the frail, wizened old woman. 'I'm Doctor Chuck . . . remember me? I just want to have a look at you and make sure you aren't getting any bedsores.'

'You won't find any bedsores on her,' Sarah barked, causing Charles to whirl around, since he hadn't been aware of her presence. Apparently she had crept up the stairs so softly that he hadn't heard her, and she was now standing in the doorway. 'I keep her clean,' she said vehemently. 'I use ointment and powder on her, and I turn her on her side every two hours the way I'm supposed to.'

'Good . . . good,' Charles said in an appeasing tone. 'You're lucky to have a daughter who loves you so much, Mary.' He took his blood pressure gauge out of his black bag. 'Now, let's see if I can pronounce you fit enough to go outside for a stroll. Would you like to go for a stroll with me?'

Mary jerked and stiffened as he was wrapping the inflatable blood pressure cuff around her emaciated arm. Shivers came over her, shimmering the folds of her long cotton nightgown. Her black eyes, sunk into pouches in her pallid, blue-veined face, bulged and dilated as her cheeks and mouth trembled.

'Great big snakes,' she rasped quaveringly. 'Great big snakes . . . a-comin' to kill us . . .'

'What kind of snakes?' Charles asked, trying for a continuation of dialogue.

But Mary wouldn't say anything more. Charles tried several different approaches, but inspired no further utterances.

'Leave her be now!' Sarah snapped. 'It's plain as the nose on your face, Doctor Chuck! All you're doin' is upsettin' her!'

'I'm sorry,' Charles said, somewhat miffed.

'Thanks for tryin' your best,' George muttered. 'We appreciate it.'

'Mind if I at least take Mary's blood pressure and pulse?' Charles ventured.

Sarah shot him an icy look, then clomped down the stairs.

'Do what you know ought to be done,' George said.

Charles used his stethoscope, tongue depressor, and blood pressure apparatus. He also did some testing and probing of Mary's reflexes, and found them even more sluggish than they had been the previous summer when he had last examined her. And her blood pressure was a bit lower. 'She's doing tolerably well,' he told George. 'There's been some decline, but that's to be expected so long as she remains an invalid. She might be able to be

19

helped more, if she were in a place equipped to deal with her problems on a daily basis.'

'Sarah won't stand for her to be put away,' George said.

'I know,' Charles commiserated, shaking his head sadly. 'The thing is, she may be right. There's no guarantee that an institution really *could* help your mother-in-law. Some people waste away even faster when they're not being cared for by their loved ones.'

'That's what Sarah says.'

'She's doing a fine job under trying circumstances.'

Sarah Stone came out onto the front porch as the two men were climbing back into the Land Rover. 'The Lord's will!' she shouted at them just before they drove away.

On the way back to Carson Manor, Charles wondered about the 'folklore' among the people of Carson Valley who were convinced that on the rare occasions when Mary Monohan was moved to speak, her words carried the weight of prophecy. He had heard the story of Tom Stone, found dead in the kitchen of a heart attack, after Mary had predicted it. She was also supposed to have talked of a 'bloody hand' three days before the postman, Jed Wise, had cut off three fingers reaching under his tractor mower to untangle a vine. Myth? Coincidence? Precognition? Charles didn't know. But he was willing to speculate that there might be something to ESP, and that a person whose conscious brain had largely stopped functioning might experience a compensatory enhancement of subconscious, extrasensory powers.

However, even if Mary Monohan happened to be such a 'gifted' person, it was hard for Charles to see how her utterances about 'great big snakes' could be anything but delirious fantasy rooted in her lifetime of fear and fascination with poisonous serpents. In spite of the fact that she had seen her own husband killed by a rattler while he was leading a snake-handling ceremony at the Carson Valley Church of Christ, she had continued to attend that church until she became an invalid. George, Sarah, and Janie still went there every Sunday. Last summer, Dr Charles Walsh had attended one of the services to write about it for a psychiatric journal.

In his opinion, the snakehandlers were motivated by something more than their strictly literal interpretation of Mark 16:18. They seemed compelled to use the deadly snakes to prove their Christian purity in a dramatic, 'irrefutable' way to all their fellow parishioners.

'If you don't trust in God,' the gaunt, bucktoothed preacher warned, 'then you better stay out of the serpent box. If you don't believe in the Lord Jesus Christ, you better stay out of the serpent box.'

'Amen! Praise the Lord!' the congregation responded.

The preacher went on, shouting, 'If you have talked about your brother – if you have been lying – if you have any terrible sins on your soul, you better stay out of the serpent box!'

The chanting started – *Jesus! Jesus! Jesus!* – as the preacher knelt and unlocked the big wooden box with holes drilled in the top so the snakes could breathe. The people who dared to handle the serpents – about fifteen of the fifty or so who were assembled in the small rural church – came forward and formed a circle. Janie and Sarah Stone stayed in their pew, but George Stone went up to take part in the ceremony. The preacher opened the lid, reached in, and pulled out a tangle of writhing, intertwined rattlers and copperheads. The chanting got louder: *Jesus! Jesus! Jesus!*

Charles Walsh was more scared than he had expected to be. He had imagined that the people would handle only one snake at a time. He nudged Sarah and asked her about this. 'One would be too *easy*,' she replied with hoarse fervour. 'The unbelievers'd scoff at *that*. But they can't say the Holy Power ain't in them who can handle so many all at once!'

Charles had brought antivenin in his doctor's bag, but had left the bag in his car. He realized that the snake-handlers wouldn't want him to bring the medicine into the church – they'd view it as an insult to their religion. But what if one of them got bitten? What would Charles do? Try to administer antivenin even if the victim didn't want it? Or stand by helplessly and watch someone die?

If one of those big timber rattlers sank its fangs into a main artery, Charles knew that he probably wouldn't even have time to go for his bag. A large dose of venom would carry directly to the heart and kill in minutes. Smaller doses injected into surface blood vessels could give antivenin a chance to prevent death. Sometimes a snake might not have much venom in its sac or might not puncture the skin very deeply; then the victim would not receive enough poison to be lethal, and the believers could say that he had been saved by an act of faith.

'Praise God!' the preacher bellowed. 'Trust in Jesus Christ! Let those with guilt on their souls *shun* these serpents!' He passed the writhing tangle to the man on his right – a lanky fellow dressed like George Stone, in plaid shirt and bibbed coveralls. The man held the snakes in both hands, letting them coil and uncoil around his wrists and forearms. Then he raised them overhead, passing them close to his face. He was perspiring heavily, but there was a beatific smile on his lips. He lowered the deadly mass of reptiles and handed them to a pale, plump lady.

She held them briefly in her trembling hands before passing them to a blonde little girl about ten years old. The child seemed naïvely unafraid, oblivious to danger. She held the heavy, squirming bundle till her arms started to lower from tiredness. The snakes made no move to strike her. 'And a little *child* shall *lead* them!' shouted the bucktoothed preacher, his deep, husky voice booming above the chanting of the congregation.

The blonde girl passed the poisonous serpents to George Stone. Charles glanced at Sarah and Janie, wondering how they would react. Janie bit her lip and squirmed, wide-eyed with fright, her prayer-clenched knuckles blanched white. Sarah knelt rigidly, almost catatonically, in the pew, fervently chanting: *Jesus! Jesus! Jesus!* Janie let out a sudden, piercing scream. A short, fat copperhead was crawling up her daddy's arm, towards his throat. 'I'm ready to die, Lord, if you want me!' George cried out. The copperhead inched closer, baring its needlelike fangs. But then it retreated and burrowed its shiny triangular head into the intertwined coils of the other snakes. George passed the writhing bundle to a frail, pretty young woman.

The circle endured. No one was bitten.

After the ceremony, George Stone told Charles, 'When the spirit is upon me, I don't have any fear of the serpents at all. They can smell fear, and that's when they're likely to strike.'

'Hmph!' Sarah scoffed. 'My daddy wasn't afraid, and *he* got bit.'

'Your daddy, Reverend Brady Monohan, died in a state of grace, doin' the Lord's work,' said the preacher. 'It's the Word of God, that's why we must carry it out. We have to go by what the Bible says. God has commanded us to take up serpents.'

'The serpents are Satan,' said Sarah. 'Satan and his minions.'

Recalling Sarah's words, Charles toyed with the possibility that Mary Monohan's prophecy might be interpreted as allegory. Was some unfathomable evil on its way? Was that what Mary subconsciously perceived? Was it what she meant by 'great big snakes a-comin' to kill us'?

3

Janie Stone hated to see the end of her day of fun and freedom. The stuff she did at the Walshes' place didn't seem like work – and she even got paid for it. She had a five-dollar bill in the pocket of her bibbed coveralls, and she patted it as she rode in her daddy's pickup. Mommy would take it off of her when she got home, but it almost didn't matter since she had had such a good time earning it.

She had groomed, watered, and fed Bullet and Lightning all by herself. Then she had helped saddle and bridle the beautiful, high-spirited palominos so Doctor Chuck and Doctor Anita could take their evening ride. Daddy had let her get up on Lightning and take him on a slow trot inside the corral. It was a sinful thought, but she wondered why, when she and Daddy were off on their own, away from Mommy and Grandma, they were about as happy as Bullet and Lightning would be if they could jump the log fence and gallop free.

Janie wished that her mother could be more like Doctor Anita – cheerful and joking and able to laugh. Then her father might not become sadder and smaller when it came time to go home. She might not have to see the light in his eyes fade, his jaws slacken, and his shoulders slump in the ten or fifteen minutes it took to drive his truck over three miles of dirt road and park it by the side of the house.

As soon as they pushed open the kitchen door, they were stabbed by one of Sarah's fiercest, coldest looks. They both glanced sheepishly down at their stockinged feet, making sure she noticed that they had left their boots – which weren't even too muddy – out on the back porch. Then they washed up and towelled off, taking picky, fussy care not to drip. 'I just waxed the floor,' Sarah snapped. 'Don't go splashing it up.'

They sat at the big, round, wooden table in the large boxlike kitchen with scarred, peeling wallpaper, chipped-up, mismatched chairs, and shiny new linoleum freshly waxed – which was the only new thing in the whole house. Sarah made Janie say Grace. Then they dug into their supper of fried pork chops, fried potatoes, and applesauce. Working at the Walshes' always made Janie hungry, so she ate a lot. So did her father. But Sarah barely touched her food. She just sat there with a stony look on her narrow, bony face. 'Janie!' she snapped. 'I don't want you wearin' tee shirts no more, you hear? You'll be thirteen years old, come September. Time you put an end to actin' like a tomboy. You're almost a woman, and it's startin' to show. I'll have to buy you the proper undergarment so's you can dress modest.'

Janie blushed, knowing that Sarah was referring to a brassiere. She hated the thought of wearing one. How could it be anything but unpleasant to be bound up in a thingamajig of cloth and metal and elastic? It seemed like she had never enjoyed her fair ration of fun in her childhood, and now her developing body was going to force her into adult encumbrances before she was ready. Petulantly, she asked, 'Can I go with Daddy to the Manor tomorrow?'

'*No*. You should know better than to ask. You've already been over there twice this week. I've got some chores I want you to do. I can't take care of Grandma and keep up with everything else around here all by myself.'

'But, Mommy, tomorrow is the day all the guests are coming.'

'All the more reason for you to stay home. You'd run over there seven days a week if'n I didn't draw the line.'

'But Doctor Chuck and Doctor Anita *want* me to come. They say I'm a good worker. I made five dollars today and – '

'You just hand that money over to me after supper. And make up your mind to prove what a good worker you are come mornin' when I put you to weedin' the garden.'

'Aw, let her come with me, Sarah,' George pleaded gently. 'Tomorrow is a-goin' to be an excitin' day for Janie. She's been lookin' forward to it. Ain't as if she gets to have a real summer vacation like most kids.'

Sarah glowered at him. 'I guess it don't bother you that she's gettin' to like the Walshes better'n she likes her own parents! They're fillin' her head with their pagan ideas, turnin' her into a heathen! So don't go against me, George, when I'm layin' the law down for my own daughter. I ain't about to forgive you for bringin' Doctor Chuck over here this afternoon without askin' me. There's nothin' no headshrinker can do for Mama – she's in the Lord's hands.'

'You know what I think, Sarah?' George said. 'I think that maybe you don't want Mama to get well 'cause then you'd have to stop thinkin' of yourself as some kind of holy martyr.'

Sarah froze soon as those words rolled off of George's tongue. He had spoken up bolder with her than he had dared to for a long time. She was so shocked and angry that her face was bloodless white, her thin lips pressed together so tight it looked like she didn't have any. But her voice was calm and icy. 'I expect that's the kind of sly drivel the headshrinkers spout off about me behind my back, George, because a hateful, sinful idea like that couldn't have come to you on your own. If it wasn't planted inside your brain by Charles and Anita Walsh, then Satan himself must've planted it.'

George's big hands clenched the table top, his green eyes locked on to Sarah's flashing brown ones. Slowly and tauntingly he said, 'We'll just have to see about *that* come Sunday.'

Janie knew that he meant to prove himself. If Satan had control of his soul, the way Mommy had accused, he could never dare to take the snakes in his hands.

'If you're so much holier than me, Sarah,' he jeered, 'how come *you* don't never come up and join the circle?'

That stunned Sarah to silence. She glowered at George for some long, slow-moving seconds, but he stared her down. She got up and scraped her pork scraps into a pie tin and wordlessly handed the tin to Janie.

Janie added her scraps and her daddy's to the pile, and went out back to feed the dog, a chained-up black mongrel named Blackie. He was already out of his doghouse, jumping up and down, whimpering and rattling his chain. Janie petted him and he jumped on her, almost knocking the pie tin out of her hands before she could set it in the dirt. She used the garden hose to fill up his water tin. Then she stayed there petting him, talking to him, and watching him eat. She wasn't anxious to go back into the house. Rather than hearing Mommy and Daddy snapping at each other, she'd sooner hear Blackie gnawing gristle and cracking bones. He was a good, tough watchdog. No stranger ever came near the house without setting him to barking and growling something fierce.

The screen door popped open, and Sarah yelled from the back porch. 'Don't just laze around with the dog! You can water the garden for me! We ain't had no rain in three days, and the soil is parched!'

'Okay, Mommy!' Janie called, trying to sound amiable.

But Sarah wasn't appeased. 'Bet the Walshes don't have to think up things to keep you busy! Bet you fall all over yourself tryin' to please them! But you don't care if you leave me all by myself takin' care of your grandma!' She glowered, then turned and went back in, banging the screen door.

Smarting from the scolding, Janie turned on the hose again and started spraying, arching the spray up in the air so it would fall like gentle rain on the young plants that were just beginning to sprout in the furrows. The weeds were coming up faster, since they were hardier and could make do with less moisture . . . but it didn't seem to Janie that the weeding needed doing so badly that it couldn't wait.

She felt guilty because what her mother had said contained a large grain of truth: she didn't like being around Grandma. Yet she had some happy memories of the old woman, even though she was only six years old when the happy things stopped. Grandma had lived with her all her life, had played with her and fed her and changed her diapers when she was a baby. She could recall Grandma carving pumpkins and baking pumpkin pies for Halloween and Thanksgiving and stringing dyed popcorn for the Christmas tree. She could also remember Grandma teaching her to be afraid of snakes, whispering to her – out of earshot of her parents – to never get to where she wanted to pick one up, even though other folks did it when they were all whipped up and talked into it by the bucktoothed preacher down at the church.

But on Sundays Janie sometimes felt an urge to go up and join the snakehandlers, to prove she was as good as anyone else. It made her proud to see Daddy taking part in the holy ceremony. After it was over and he was safe, she felt giddy and thrilled all over, even though while the poisonous snakes were squirming in his hands she always thought she would die from fright and anxiety.

Doctor Chuck had asked her what her thoughts and feelings were, and she had told him. Like Grandma, he had tried to discourage her from giving in to her desire to handle serpents. But if it was in the Bible, how could it be the wrong thing to do?

Sarah never told Janie not to handle the snakes, even though she never did it herself because of seeing her own daddy die that way. If she knew Doctor Chuck had spoken against the ceremony, it would give her even more grounds for calling him a heathen. But Janie wondered: If the Walshes were such terrible people for not going to the Carson Valley Church of Christ or any other church on Sundays – then why were they so much fun to be with, so smart and kind and cheerful, when Sarah was so bitter and unhappy? It wasn't easy for Janie to believe the explanation that had been drilled into her – that evil, sinful people get their reward in *this* world, and God-fearing people are rewarded in the hereafter. Doctor Chuck and Doctor Anita didn't seem evil and sinful. They were too darned nice.

Janie noticed that the sun was going down and the sky off in the distance, above the thick woods, was streaked red. The red sky meant it wouldn't rain tomorrow. It would be a lovely day for the guests to arrive at Carson Manor. But she would be weeding the garden, missing out on all the excitement. The only spark of glamour in her young life came from her association with the Walshes, and when she was deprived of it, her everyday existence seemed unbearably gloomy and drab.

She was scared to go against the way she had been brought up. Ashamed to admit to herself that she wanted to learn to be more like Doctor Anita and Doctor Chuck than like her own folks. She had the highest grades in her class in the Carson Valley Junior-Senior High School. She was especially good at English composition and had been asked to help on the school newspaper, but Mommy wouldn't let her. The Walshes thought that was a shame. They said she should keep studying hard and maybe win a scholarship to go to college. Sometimes she fantasized about living with them in Richmond while she attended the university there. With them to help her and be almost like her substitute parents, she wouldn't be so scared of the big city.

She stopped moving the hose nozzle back and forth and let the spray fall all in one place, while she looked down at her chest. She realized that what her mother had said was quite true: she was changing into a woman. Come September she'd be a teenager, in the eighth grade. But graduating from high school, and starting college – if she could ever make it that far – was still five years away.

It seemed like a terribly long time to study and struggle and keep alive the near-impossible hope of escaping from Carson Valley.

4

In the mellowness of twilight, Charles and Anita Walsh tethered their horses by Carson Creek, which bordered their fifty-acre estate. The shallow, fast-moving water gurgled and sparkled over its bed of flat rock, and the reddening sky could be glimpsed through the surrounding trees. Charles and Anita felt at peace sitting on the bank, breathing the cool air of a June evening, and listening to Bullet and Lightning snorting occasionally while they munched tall grass.

'We can't stay here too long,' Anita said regretfully. 'It'll soon be too dark to see.'

'No problem,' said Charles. 'We won't have to pick our way through the woods to get home. Just lead the horses along the creek till we reach the dirt road.'

She snuggled up to him, feeling warm and protected as he put his arm around her. 'Still,' she said, 'we ought to be heading back early. Tomorrow we'll be up to our ears again in other people's problems . . . so if you have any designs on this amply endowed Victorian body of mine . . .'

He kissed her, letting her know that he did indeed have designs for later. Then they sat back, holding each other, admiring the fading sunset and enjoying the tranquillity of their summer retreat.

'It's a darn shame in a way,' Anita murmured.

'What is?'

'We get more out of it than the folks who've paid their dues. The people who've grown up in the valley don't see its beauty anymore. All they see is the poverty and harshness of trying to make a living from old, worn-out

31

farms. You and I are usurpers. We don't work the soil, but we live better than those who do.'

'We're the patricians,' Charles joked. Then, more soberly, he said, 'I don't think the valley folks hate their lives so much. Otherwise they'd leave. They cling to what they have here because they *do* love it. The valley is in their blood. They see the beauty of it, all right – they just wish they could make it pay, like it once did.'

'Janie Stone wants to get away to Richmond,' said Anita.

'Well, she should,' said Charles. 'She should broaden her horizons, and then maybe someday she'll want to come back.'

'Yes, and handle snakes,' Anita jibed.

'And be the high priestess of the snake cult,' Charles chuckled.

'I truly doubt that Janie will ever want to see the valley again if she succeeds in breaking away from it,' said Anita.

'Oh, I don't know. You admitted you didn't appreciate it in your girlhood, but now you do.'

'Living at Carson Manor is a far cry from living in a drafty, ramshackle old place with a leaky tin roof. Besides, I didn't grow up in the valley, I only came to visit a few times. For me it was never a kind of pastoral prison, like it is for poor Janie. She's a bright young girl, but if she stays around here the bible-thumpers will ruin her. George Stone is a darn nice fellow in most ways, but what kind of role model is he – showing his daughter that it's somehow righteous, virtuous, and . . . and *glorious* to handle poisonous snakes? Does he want her to die like Sarah's father did?'

'I've told Janie what you and I think of the snake-handling,' Charles said. 'I've tried to subtly discourage her from giving in to the emotional pressure and going up and trying to prove something when everybody around her is all psyched up and chanting and so on.'

'She respects us, so we have a responsibility to try to influence her in a healthier direction,' Anita agreed. 'But we'd better watch ourselves or Sarah Stone will start believing we're Satan's minions.'

'I think she believes it already,' Charles laughed.

'We're not going to find it so funny,' Anita said, 'if one of these nights the good valley folk storm Carson Manor and burn us at the stake.'

'A sobering thought,' said Charles.

The sky was lead grey with a halo of silver fanning the tops of the Shenandoah foothills when they untethered their horses and led them out to the dirt road. Here the bright three-quarter moon poking through the trees was sufficient to navigate by, and they mounted up for the ride back to the corral, where they unsaddled and unbridled Bullet and Lightning.

The Manor was quiet, but there were night lights on. Apparently, Brenda and Meredith Meachum had retired to their rooms. Charles and Anita had arranged for the two servants to stay on the premises for the summer; the rest of the year they lived in Carsonville where they both worked in the cafeteria of the Carson Valley Junior-Senior High School.

Charles wandered through the kitchen, dining room, library, and study, taking pleasure in the antebellum furnishings and stealing this opportunity to have the lovely old rooms to himself before being swamped by the expediencies of the guests who would arrive tomorrow for the marriage encounter. When he went up to the master bedroom, he could hear water running; Anita was in their private bathroom taking her shower. He turned on the television set, an incongruous apparatus in a decor that was almost completely pre-Civil War. The nine o'clock news was on, and Charles figured he might as well find out what was going on in the outside world, because over the next four days – from Thursday to Sunday – he would have few opportunities of doing so.

The majority of the newscast was devoted to an episode of terrorism that had become a major media event in New York City. A gang of radicals calling themselves the Green Brigade were holed up inside the Manhattan National Bank with fourteen hostages. According to a reporter on the scene, the terrorists had already grabbed over two million dollars from the bank vault, and they were now demanding the release from Attica Correctional Facility of some of their cohorts, principally their leader, 'General Kintay'. The terrorist in charge of the bank raid was Kintay's mistress, a tough, shrill fanatic calling herself 'Colonel Mao'. At one point she appeared in close-up, holding a big ugly pistol at a bank officer's head. She made a speech loaded with Marxist platitudes and feverish predictions of 'the ultimate defeat and collapse of the United States Empire'.

Charles shook his head despairingly, listening to her venomous diatribe. A tall, wiry, pimpled blonde, she was wearing a bright green beret, camouflage fatigues, and – one item that particularly startled Charles – a white armband with the emblem of the green brigade: a coiled green serpent baring its fangs.

Charles thought it was a good thing he wasn't super-stitious because serpents seemed to be cropping up in his life today like a bad omen.

When he heard the shower stop running behind the closed bathroom door, he shut off the TV so Anita wouldn't have her day ruined by the news broadcast. He thought to himself that he'd rather handle real snakes like the ones in the valley than the ones he had just seen on the news. And he basked in appreciation of how fortunate he was to be able to withdraw and refresh his spirit at an unspoiled sanctuary like Carson Manor, snug and safe from the hideously irrational terrors of the modern world.

But that night, after he and Anita had made love, he didn't fall into a peaceful sleep. He found himself tossing and turning, with a sense of edginess and dread that had no logical basis. He got a few hours of fitful rest before sheer exhaustion sucked him down into deeper slumber, and his dreams evolved into a nightmare . . .

He saw himself peeling back a heavy shroud of decayed, rotting bedcovers to reveal Mary Monohan's frail, pasty body caked with oozing, bleeding bedsores. The invalid arose to lead him by the hand, and he followed her with heartsick unwillingness, stepping in the ooze that dripped from her chafed wounds. She took him to a church crawling with serpents, hanging from the windows, the steeple, and the eaves like a live net of writhing terror. Then he saw that the snakes were people. All of the congregation – the farmers, the coal miners, the children, and the housewives – had the bodies of snakes growing out of their necks, and the fat, green, scaly necks were so long that the heads of the snakes slithered on the floor or climbed in coils to the rafters, baring their poison-dripping fangs and their forked, vibrating tongues.

Charles screamed, trying with all his might to turn and run. For an eternity of time, he could not move. His legs felt like lead, and Mary Monohan kept grinning at him with her snaky eyes, and she wouldn't let go of his hand.

He woke up screaming, in a cold sweat. When he realized it had been only a dream, he still wondered why Anita hadn't been jarred awake. But she was sleeping peacefully, a slight smile on her face. His loud screaming must have been only in his head.

He tried to push the nightmare back into his subconscious, but he wasn't very successful. He must have lain awake for at least another hour. Finally he managed to get a couple of hours of heavy, dreamless sleep before the alarm went off. He let Anita use the bathroom first, so he could lie in bed for a while longer. Then, after she went downstairs, he felt compelled to turn on the seven A.M. news.

The hostage crisis in New York was still going on. Charles had hoped that by this time it would be over, without casualties, and with the authorities firmly in control. He never liked to see man's worst side triumph, and he realized that his nightmare had been a manifestation of that fear. It would have put his mind at ease if he could have found out that the real-life situation had ended better than his dream. But so far that wasn't the case.

According to the TV commentator, some of the Green Brigade demands had already been met. An airport bus had been provided for the terrorists and their hostages, and it was parked at the side of the Manhattan National Bank. A Boeing 747 was waiting to take them to Cuba. But General Kintay and his jailed cronies had not been released from Attica. Apparently, Colonel Mao had been told that she and her band could go to Cuba with two million dollars, but without Kintay. She had demanded to be allowed to go on television to give her answer.

Luridly fascinated and appalled, Charles watched as, once again, Colonel Mao appeared in close-up with her gun at the bank official's head. With a tough sneer on her pimpled face, she announced that she would not wait past ten o'clock. At that hour, and every half hour thereafter, one hostage would be 'executed' – until General Kintay and his 'comrades in capitalist chains' were released and safely delivered inside the bank. Then the Green Brigade soldiers and their 'prisoners of war' must be permitted to proceed unharmed to LaGuardia Airport to board the jetliner which would fly them to 'a rendezvous of destiny with Comrade Fidel'.

When Anita called him and told him his eggs were getting cold, Charles clicked the TV off and went downstairs. Putting on a cheerful smile for his wife, he kissed her good morning. He exchanged wisecracks with Brenda and Meredith Meachum, who were bustling around in the huge kitchen, kneading biscuit dough and cutting up vegetables for the big supper that would be laid out for this afternoon's guests. Normally Charles enjoyed the anticipation and the pleasant excitement of a busy day getting underway. But today he couldn't truly relax, and he didn't know why. He told himself it couldn't be the news broadcast. Horrible things were always happening in the world, and one had to forget about them so long as they weren't happening near at hand. Carson Manor was the ideal place for pushing the world's ills out of one's mind.

After breakfast, he and Anita went to their study to review the case files of the patients who were scheduled to show up for the marriage encounter. But Charles's concentration wasn't up to par.

'What's the matter, dear?' Anita finally asked, taking off her reading glasses to peer at him quizzically.

'Nothing,' he told her. 'I just didn't sleep well last night.'

'Are you kidding?' she laughed. 'When the alarm went off you were dead to the world.'

'Well, when I finally dropped off, I was totally exhausted, after tossing and turning most of the night. I think I'll take Lightning out for a little ride before lunch. Maybe it'll help me perk up.'

He thought of telling his wife about his nightmare, just to get it off his chest. But why burden her with something so ugly and unsettling? She'd only tell him to push it out of his mind. It didn't mean anything of any deep psychological significance. He had only dreamed it because yesterday there had been too much talk about snakes.

5

Jim Spencer, the baggy-eyed, hatchet-faced commander of the FBI SWAT team surrounding the Manhattan National Bank, rumpled his sweaty fingers through his iron-grey crewcut as he talked on the phone with Colonel Mao. He was in a drugstore across from the bank, where he had established his command post. Ever since Mao had issued her televised ultimatum, Spencer had been on the phone with either her or the governor of New York. All night long, the governor had been insisting that he would never consent to the release of any prisoners from Attica. Now he had finally changed his mind. But Mao didn't believe it. In five more minutes, unless Spencer could convince her otherwise, she would order the death of one of the hostages.

Spencer was seething with frustration. He'd dearly love to send the Green Brigade and all others of their ilk into oblivion. He had no stomach for 'negotiating' with them – it made him feel like a coward and a pimp. Which is how Colonel Mao wanted him to feel.

When she had first taken over the bank, at three o'clock yesterday afternoon, she had telephoned the FBI's Manhattan office. She had made it clear that she would deal only with Jim Spencer, her hated adversary. For nine months he had been trying to nail her, ever since she had escaped the trap that had put her lover, General Kintay, in prison. Now she was humiliating the FBI man by making him kowtow to her insane demands.

During the past nineteen hours, while he was pretending to give in, item by item – lining up TV time for Mao, then food and drink, then an airport coach, then an airplane, then more TV time – he had been trying to get permission from the national director of the FBI and the governor of New York simply to let his SWAT team launch an attack. If terrorists and hostages alike had to die, so be it. It would be a bitter price to pay. But Spencer was convinced that insurgencies of this sort would cease only when the perpetrators were consistently shown that they could never hope to gain anything from their despicable acts.

He had thought that the permission to attack would be granted once Mao made the threat to start executing hostages. If the governor was bound and determined not to release any prisoners, then the only other choice would be to go in shooting. Spencer had caustically pointed this out. And the governor had ultimately knuckled under – to the terrorists. The FBI director had ordered Spencer not to attack as long as most of the hostages could still be saved. A helicopter was on its way to Attica to pick up Kintay and the other Green Brigade inmates. But it was almost ten o'clock now. And Colonel Mao was refusing to back off of her deadline.

As he clutched the phone, the ash from a chain-smoked cigarette tumbled down the front of Spencer's sweat-stained shirt. He flung the butt from his mouth and stomped on it, grinding black streaks into the grey tile floor. Talking urgently but trying not to convey panic, he said, 'You must understand . . . Colonel . . . that I'm not in absolute control of all the decisions. I had to wait to hear from the governor of New York. Even though Kintay and the others were arrested by the FBI, they were tried for murder under the laws of this state, rather than for their Federal offences. The governor had to make the decision to release them. Then he had to arrange for the helicopter and – '

'Pig!' Colonel Mao shrilled. 'Don't give me that bullshit! I'm sick of your stalling!'

Spencer held the receiver away from his stinging eardrum. His ulcer was burning worse than when he tried to communicate with his own incorrigible, sixteen-year-old daughter. He wondered to what extent Caroline might ultimately defy and disgrace him, and he hoped she wouldn't go as far as the crazy bitch he was now talking to.

Like the daughter that Spencer was worried about, Colonel Mao was from an American middle-class family. Her real name was Denise Schaeffer. At the University of California at Berkeley, her rebellion against her parents evolved into rebellion against society. She drifted on the fringes of the Symbionese Liberation Army, hobnobbed with Nancy 'Fahizah' Perry and Patricia 'Zoya' Soltysik, and distributed pamphlets extolling the kidnapping of Patty Hearst and the ransom demand of 'food for the masses'. When the SLA was virtually wiped out in a fiery holocaust in Los Angeles, it transformed Denise Schaeffer from a Marxist sympathizer to a hardened zealot. She abandoned her teenage husband and her baby boy to become the mistress of a black man – Wilson Woodruff, alias General Kintay – who had been a prison mate of the SLA's slain leader, Donald DeFreeze, alias General Cinque. Denise denounced her family, her church, and her country to become a 'revolutionary soldier' in Woodruff's Green Brigade – an SLA splinter group. She was wanted by the FBI and the New York State Police as an accomplice in the same crimes that had put her comrades in prison: the attempted hijacking of an armoured truck and the gunning down of two state troopers.

'Time is running out, pig,' she warned Jim Spencer. 'In three more minutes I will order the first execution.'

'Colonel, there's no need to do that,' Spencer said, stroking her ego by addressing her with her self-bestowed military title. He tried to keep his voice calm and soothing while he fumbled frantically for another cigarette. 'As I

40

told you, Colonel, the governor has consented to the release of your people. But this kind of thing takes time. It has to go through proper channels. You can't – '

'Don't tell me what I can't do!' Colonel Mao snarled. '*I'm* in command here! I speak for all oppressed people! I know all too well that other assaults on the Establishment have failed in the past because the guerrillas didn't adhere with unwavering commitment to their strategy and objectives. As long as I give you mere *talk*, you won't respect me. So now I'm giving you action. In three more minutes we will execute one of our prisoners of war.'

'Don't you honour the Geneva Convention? How can you call yourself the champion of the people if you kidnap and kill them at random, without any regard for their individual merits or their innocence?'

'No one is completely innocent in this world,' said Mao. 'We have interviewed the prisoners and have selected the first one to die. More executions will follow. One every half hour until General Kintay and our other comrades are delivered safely to us.'

'They're on their way!' Spencer yelled. 'Please don't do anything rash! I assure – '

The connection was broken with a loud click, shocking him with the realization that his pleas were going to be ignored. He stared at the phone, then hung up. He dug in his pockets to find some matches and lit his cigarette, sucking at it madly in short gulps. He picked up the phone again and started to dial, hoping to re-establish contact with Colonel Mao before the execution that she had promised could take place. His ears were cocked for the sound of a bullet from across the street – but that sound didn't come. Instead a SWAT surveillance man yelled –

'They're opening the front door! One of the hostages is coming out!'

Spencer slammed the phone down and strode swiftly to

the front of the drugstore and through the wide-open glass doors. Behind a sandbag barricade, the khaki-uniformed SWAT men were deployed with their rifles and machine guns. Peering cautiously above the fortification, Spencer saw the released hostage in the glare of morning sunlight – a plump middle-aged man in a three-piece brown suit. He was trembling as he walked across the street with his hands up. Then the front door of the bank opened a crack – there was a metallic gleam and a loud twang – and the man screamed, buckled, and fell.

'Hold your fire!' Spencer yelled as the front door of the bank was pulled tightly shut. If the SWAT men didn't control their urge to start shooting, the rest of the hostages might die right here and now. Spencer almost wished they would disobey him, and the devil take the consequences. But no shots rang out.

Writhing in agony, the man in the brown suit was trying to crawl towards the curb. Spencer sent a couple of SWAT men, ducking and weaving, to help the downed hostage to safety. They half dragged, half carried him behind the pile of sandbags, where he collapsed groaning, a shiny steel shaft sticking out of his blood-streaked thigh.

'A crossbow bolt!' one of the SWAT men exclaimed.

'Missed its mark!' said another SWAT man. 'He's going to live.'

But Spencer had his doubts. He remembered the trade-mark of the SLA: bullets tipped with cyanide. 'Stretcher! *Stretcher!*' he yelled to the police doctors and paramedics who had set up an emergency station in the rear of the drugstore.

But before the medics came to help, the man who had been shot with the crossbow shuddered, convulsed, and died. Spencer knelt and pulled the steel bolt from the man's thigh. It was a hollow shaft. When the FBI man tilted the shaft downwards, a few drops of a yellowish liquid oozed out. It wasn't cyanide, or it would've smelled like bitter almonds.

The phone started ringing back in the drugstore, and Spencer ran to grab it. Colonel Mao's demented laugh shrilled in his ear.

'Rattlesnake venom!' she told him, still laughing, as if it were the punch line of a joke.

6

Janie Stone was weeding the garden and keeping her ears cocked for the sound of her daddy's pickup truck. She was sweating in the blazing sun, which was almost directly overhead, so it must be nearly noon. Daddy ought to be coming home for lunch.

Janie laid down her hoe and went to pet Blackie, the chained-up watchdog. On her way, she cast a glance towards the house, not wanting to get caught sneaking herself a break. She felt sorry for herself for not being at Carson Manor and for having to do such a boring chore. 'Darn!' she said out aloud, wiping her brow. She wasn't allowed to wear tee shirts anymore, or else she would've felt a lot cooler. She was wearing regular jeans instead of bibbed ones, and a short-sleeved, blue plaid blouse. Funny, the blouse made her feel more like a little girl than a tee shirt would've because it was so baggy it gave no hint of her developing breasts.

As she petted Blackie, he kept whimpering and jumping up on her, then running towards the house till his chain clanked and jerked his neck. He was hungry. He always knew when it was close to feeding time and always acted like he never got fed.

The screen door banged open, and Janie quickly stopped fooling with the dog and went back to using her hoe. But Mommy didn't yell at her. Instead she came walking across the back yard.

'Janie,' Sarah Stone said. 'Grandma won't eat nothin' again. I made cornbread and lentil soup – used to be her favourite – but she won't take none from me. I want you to try and feed it to her.'

'But . . .' Janie gestured at the work that still remained to be done in the garden, hoping it would save her from having to feed her grandma.

'Don't give me no buts,' Sarah said sternly. 'Mama always did moon and fawn over you, more'n she did me when I was a child. Maybe she'll cotton to *you* feedin' her – and if'n she does, it can be *your* chore from now on.'

Rubbing her hands on her jeans, Janie went dejectedly into the house. If she had to feed Grandma all the time, she'd never, ever get to go to the Manor. It took so long. And it was worse than feeding a baby. The food kept dribbling down Grandma's chin, and you had to keep wiping it up. And when the old lady opened her pale, pink mouth, you saw her yellow, rotten teeth with strings of saliva connecting them like glistening spider webs.

Janie took her good old time washing her hands, being exceedingly careful not to splash or drip. Then, with slow reluctance, like a prisoner walking the last mile, she climbed the stairs to Grandma's bedroom to be enveloped by the sour, sick smell that always reminded her of someone dying.

Buried under a patchwork quilt, even though the room was as stuffy as a tomb, Mary Monohan had her wrinkled, skull-like head tilted towards her grandchild. Her thin, white lips were parted slightly in a ghastly, unencouraging smile.

The cornbread and lentil soup and a cup of sassafras tea were on a tray on the seat of an old ladderbacked chair next to the bed. Janie picked up the tray and sat down, then took up the spoon. 'Hi, Grandma,' she said, trying hard to sound cheerful. 'This lentil soup really smells good, doesn't it? Want me to give you some?'

Grandma opened her mouth, her hollow cheeks trembling with the effort. Janie averted her eyes, dipping the spoon to pick up a few lentils and a shallow tidbit of brown broth.

'Too late . . . it's too . . . late . . . child . . .'

At the totally unexpected sound of her grandma's weak, scratchy voice, Janie dropped the spoon on the tray. She stared into the sunken but wildly gleaming black eyes. Then, remembering what Doctor Chuck had said about trying to keep Grandma talking if she ever once *started* to talk, Janie stammered, 'W-what's too late, Grandma?'

The old lady sprung at the little girl with sudden ferociousness, grabbing her by the wrists, sending the tray full of food crashing to the floor.

'It's too *late*, child! Run! *Run!* Great big *snakes!* On their way . . . a-comin' to *kill* us!'

7

Dr Charles Walsh turned Lightning loose in the corral and went into the house to wash up. He could've done it in the kitchen, but Brenda and Meredith were so busy in there, with both sinks and all the counter space tied up, that he decided he'd better not get in their way. So he went upstairs to use his and Anita's private bathroom – and also, while he was at it, to change into a fresh shirt.

He couldn't resist turning on the TV. Normally, on the days when the marriage encounters were about to get underway, he could ignore television, but today it seemed to be luring him like a magnet. The hostage crisis in New York was still on his mind, as if it had some perverse connection with his own life – though he didn't really believe that. No direct connection, he told himself, even if it had helped to instigate his bad dream. Still, he couldn't fight down the urge to watch the noon news.

He learned, to his horror, that a hostage had been killed by a hollowed-out crossbow bolt filled with rattlesnake venom. Thirty minutes later, another hostage had been shot in the abdomen with a cyanide-tipped bullet that had produced a slow, agonizing death. And a third hostage would have died if the helicopter carrying General Kintay and his cohorts hadn't arrived from Attica just a minute and a half before the end of the next half-hour interval.

Disbelieving his own eyes, Charles watched the helicopter land in the middle of Manhattan and discharge a gang of murderers, twenty-four strong. Hordes of policemen and SWAT specialists on rooftops and behind barricades were powerless to use their weapons as the newly arrived villains joined the ones inside the bank. Charles Walsh kept expecting all hell to break loose. But it didn't. Everybody held their fire.

A TV camera zoomed in on Wilson Woodruff – General Kintay. Like a celebrity with nothing to fear from his legions of adoring fans, he paused by the bank entrance, raising his arm in a clenched-fist salute. There was an abrupt cut back to the studio commentator who said that, upon being released from his prison cell, General Kintay had demanded that he be allowed to give a nationally televised speech to 'the enslaved masses of the United States Empire'. One of the three major networks had yielded to Kintay's wishes, hoping to prevent the deaths of additional hostages. The terrorist leader would go on camera at approximately three o'clock.

Charles marvelled at how extremely media-conscious all the maniacs were these days. They didn't feel important – perhaps didn't even feel they existed – until they got on television. Because TV had done their thinking for them all their lives, whatever happened on the box was more real to them than their own thoughts.

Kintay was getting all the ego-stroking his warped mind might desire. Using a montage of grammar-school and high-school yearbook photos, police mug shots, and pictures of Kintay's friends, family members, and accomplices, the TV commentator was presenting a detailed biographical profile.

Wilson Woodruff, aka General Kintay, was a product of the Watts ghetto of Los Angeles, but he was only thirteen years old in 1965 when the riots and 'torching' took place there, and by his own admission he did not take part except as a looter. During his teens he wasn't terribly political or radical. His assaults on society were motivated by self-interest. He was a mugger, burglar, and drug pusher. Busted on a narcotics charge in 1972, he was sentenced to three years in Vacaville, where he came under the influence of Donald 'General Cinque' DeFreeze and other black Marxists, who made him recognize his evil and immoral ways and caused him to undergo a soul-searching personality transformation. He had been a parasite, an exploiter, and now he wanted to be saviour of the people. In prison he became for the first time an avid, if spotty, reader. He evolved an ideology that was an eclectic mishmash of Karl Marx, Huey Newton, Malcolm X, and assorted smatterings of pop culture. He began to acquire followers, whom he lumped together under what he called 'the Green Brigade' – because he espoused a militant approach to 'the greening of America'. His *nom de guerre*, Kintay, was a phonetic spelling of Kinte, as in Kunta Kinte, the powerful African character in Alex Haley's book, *Roots*. Apparently, Woodruff saw himself as an indomitable reincarnation of the slave who had refused to let slavery conquer him.

Immediately following the profile of Kintay, there was a reporter-on-the-scene interview with a fellow named Jim Spencer, who had been negotiating with the terrorists in his capacity as commander of the FBI SWAT team. Spencer fended off some tough questions by insisting that his job was to save innocent lives, and all other concerns were secondary to that. He admitted that the Green Brigade and their hostages were going to be allowed to go to Cuba. A jetliner was waiting for them at LaGuardia.

Charles thought of Mary Monohan's 'premonition'. The Green Brigade terrorists, figuratively speaking, were behaving like 'great big snakes'. But they were in New York, bound for Havana, miles away. Their flight path would probably take them over Virginia. Could this be what Mary Monohan sensed? Intellectually, Charles rejected the notion. He could stretch his imagination to allow for the faint possibility that the aged invalid might from time to time exhibit some subtle manifestations of clairvoyancy. But it seemed absurd to suppose that the impending movement of a plane over the land, like a hand inching across a ouija board, could send out a strong enough signal to disturb Mary's psychic antenna, assuming she had one.

After the interview with the SWAT commander, a catfood commercial came on the TV. Three Siamese cats were singing a barbershop harmony. That was quite enough for Charles. He shut the set off and went to join Anita for lunch on the veranda.

8

To Charles and Anita's surprise, the first couple to arrive for the marriage encounter were Mark and Heather Pearson. The Walshes were barely done eating when the Pearsons' snazzy red sports car zipped on to the driveway, Heather behind the wheel. Knowing Mark's attitude about psychotherapy, Charles and Anita might've expected him to balk at showing up early, and perhaps not to show up at all.

Mark Pearson was the only one of the expected guests whom the psychiatrists had never met. Charles had been seeing Heather as a regular patient back in Richmond, without any cooperation from her husband. Mark was apparently too proud to admit that he and his wife needed professional help. Charles had told Heather about Carson Manor, with the idea that Mark might be persuaded to come, if he could look at it more as a vacation than as therapy. Hopefully, once he was exposed to the benefits of counselling, his resistance might abate and he might consent to joint sessions after he and his wife went back to Richmond.

The Walshes were so enamoured of Carson Manor that they had inordinate faith in its ability to charm other people. They were not disappointed by Heather's initial reaction. 'Oh! It's so lovely here!' she enthused as she and Mark got out of their car after parking it in the brick courtyard. But he remained noncommittal, casting a wary, probing gaze on Charles and Anita, who were coming down from the veranda.

Mark and Heather Pearson were at first glance quite a

handsome young couple, till one saw that Mark's strapping, dark-haired good looks were spoiled by sullenness, and Heather's natural blonde beauty was diffused by the sad, troubled look in her pale blue eyes. He was a struggling painter and sculptor, and she was a highly successful commercial artist. In her sessions with Dr Charles Walsh, Heather had insisted that her husband was far more talented than she; yet she was the one making a substantial income, free-lancing for advertising agencies, while he was trying to turn out enough good, 'serious' work to interest one of the top galleries in sponsoring him. Meantime, he was ashamed of needing his wife's financial support and bitter at the world for not recognizing his genius. Underneath the bitterness were festering self-doubts that had lately led to bouts of sexual impotence. Heather constantly tried to reassure Mark that his work was so good it was bound to start selling, and even if it didn't happen for a long time she would still love him. But apparently he was afraid that in the long run a woman as beautiful and resourceful as his wife would not stick with a 'failure'.

Trying to keep her voice light and carefree, Heather introduced her husband to Anita and Charles. Mark was wearing faded jeans, beat-up sockless sneakers, and a yellow tee shirt with black block letters that said JOE'S BAR. Heather was tan and lovely in red shorts and a red-and-white halter. Shaking Mark's rough, strong hand, Charles said, 'Well! You certainly have the grip of a sculptor! Heather tells me your work is marvellous.'

'So far not many of the right people think so,' said Mark, kicking at a tuft of grass wedged between the bricks of the courtyard. Then, with humourless and unconvincing bravado, he added, 'But I'm going to change their minds.'

'Of course you will, honey,' said Heather, smiling encouragingly and putting her hand on his shoulder.

But he gave her a petulant stare. 'What's the matter, babe? Tired of being the only successful one in the family?'

For a moment she looked as if she might cry. But Anita picked up the beat of the conversation, trying to give her a chance to recover. 'You two must've made good time. It usually takes *us* about five hours to drive here from Richmond.'

Just then Meredith Meachum popped out on to the veranda – a plump and sturdy young black woman, on her way to becoming as fat as her mother. Like Brenda, she was wearing one of the white uniforms they both wore when they worked in the school cafeteria in Carsonville. She poked her head around a pillar and called out, 'Doctor Chuck! Will you be needin' me to help carry the luggage?'

'No, that's okay, Meredith, we'll handle it!' Charles told her, and she shook her head disapprovingly at his refusal to let her do her job. Then she started to pick up the dishes from lunch.

Noticing this, Heather said, 'My goodness! Are we too early! You must've just finished eating.'

'Makes no difference,' said Charles, smiling graciously. He didn't want Mark to feel uncomfortable and skip out.

'I'm sorry,' Heather said apologetically. 'I thought you said any time after noon. Since this *is* sort of a little vacation for me and Mark, we decided to drive as far as Charlottesville yesterday afternoon. Do you believe both of us have lived in Virginia all our lives and had never seen Monticello? And it's right outside Charlottesville, so we chose that route. Yesterday we took the historical tour, then had a nice dinner in a country inn that's been in operation since before the Civil War. Then this morning we had a late breakfast at the motel and drove straight here, allowing time to get lost – but your directions were so accurate we didn't miss a single turn. That's why we're here already.'

'Fine with us!' Anita beamed. 'Why don't we help you with your stuff and show you up to your room? Then you can join us for some coffee – or Charles's favourite, a mint julep – on the vernada, and we'll just relax while we wait for the other guests.'

'What did you think of Monticello, Mark?' Charles asked as they started unloading the trunk of the sports car.

'Absolutely beautiful,' the aspiring artist replied. 'No wonder Thomas Jefferson didn't want to leave it to become president. It's too bad we can't all live like that – but it's an ideal that's becoming less attainable nowadays, instead of more so.'

'Carson Manor is our little attempt at it,' said Charles with restrained pride. 'I think you'll enjoy yourself here, Mark. We're glad to have you.'

Charles always tried to be optimistic about his patients, and so he took heart in the fact that Mark Pearson had expressed an appreciation for Monticello that matched his own, and that he felt was in keeping with the finer sensibilities Mark was supposed to possess. Maybe he was a troubled young man, but Charles had a hunch that Heather could be right: the young man could be salvageable.

However, he might have scaled his optimism downwards if he could have observed the couple when they were alone in their room. It was in the rear of the house, on the second storey, where its large windows brought in sunshine and fresh air that billowed the filmy white curtains. The airy, sunshiny feeling was enhanced by the white walls and ceiling with white trim and wainscoting. Between two of the windows was a dark mahogany *escritoire* with brass fittings, which matched the tall, elegant chest of drawers against the adjacent wall. In front of the fireplace were two comfortable-looking

54

padded chairs, and between them a Queen Anne table. The dominant piece of furniture was the high, plump, four-poster bed, its canopy and spread done in the same rococo-patterned green satin with gold fringe that had been used on the drapes.

Charles and Anita had told each other that this room was ideal for a young couple who were in effect striving to capture the mood of a second honeymoon. Like the rest of Carson Manor, it was a retreat from the twentieth century. It could almost seem absurd to have modern anxiety problems in a setting like this.

'I think it's a perfectly lovely room, don't you, honey?' Heather said, folding some garments into a drawer.

Mark was lying flat on his back on top of the bed, while Heather did all their unpacking. The two suitcases were opened up next to him, and he had barely budged to make room for them.

'Lovely, lovely,' he mocked sarcastically. 'You're just like the shrinks. You're under the delusion that coming here is going to make everything wonderful between us, like rubbing a magic lamp – when what's really wrong is not something we can change like the scenery.'

A chill of dread shot up Heather's spine. Was he going to tell her that he no longer loved her? Losing his love was her deepest fear. She could cope with the rest: his moodiness, his anger, his despair. But please don't let him turn against her the way he seemed to have turned against himself.

'You told Dr Walsh you liked the room,' she reminded him, biting her lip.

'I was being polite to our host,' he said acidly. 'Our *rich* host. Sure it's a nice room – it ought to be, for what we're forking out. A thousand dollars for a four-day fiasco! All we're doing is helping the Walshes get richer. We really *ought* to have our heads examined for letting them treat us like snot-nosed little kids at a summer camp.'

'We can afford it,' Heather said. 'I'm making good money this year. Last week I got that check from – '

'I'm sick and tired of hearing about how much you make!' Mark snapped.

'I consider it our money, not just mine,' Heather defended.

'Then why are you always throwing it up in my face?' He swung his legs off the bed and sat up, glowering at her.

She came over and sat beside him, feeling contrite. 'Who earns the most money means nothing to me,' she said, 'as long as we're both happy. You have to believe me, Mark, it's how I've always felt. I'm supposed to be taking the financial burden off of you, so you can concentrate on your work. I've never complained about it, have I?'

'Not in so many words, no.'

'Not in actions either.'

'You think I'm crazy,' he sneered. 'It's all in my head, right?'

'I think you're down on yourself because you're not getting the recognition you deserve. But please don't take it out on the people around you, Mark. I'll stick with you, I promise. But please don't take it out on *me*.'

He didn't answer her. He didn't give her any reassurance at all. After a while, she got up and continued unpacking. It was a cheerless task, plagued by thoughts that her husband might be falling out of love with her.

She was desperate for this marriage encounter to work. Not that she thought it would be some kind of cure-all, as Mark had implied, but that it might open him up to her again. Then they could both work to let in more light.

Yesterday, even though he hadn't tried to make love to her, he had acted as though he still cared. Today he was being nasty to her again. Her patched-up hopes seemed to be coming apart at the seams. She dreaded the thought that her five-year marriage, which had started out so bravely and wonderfully, might end in divorce.

Was it her fault for being so good at holding up her end of the bargain? Was it fatal for a woman to earn more than her man?

As long as she had known Mark, she had brought home a fatter paycheque. It wasn't supposed to bother him. It was part of their game plan. She had agreed with him that she should be the prime breadwinner till his career could take off, as they both knew it would if he were given a decent chance. Heather looked upon herself as not only his wife, but his help-mate, his patron. She was willing to do whatever was necessary to pave the way for his talent.

In the beginning he had seemed so bold, so free, so uninhibited – a modern privateer plying stone and canvas. Money just wasn't one of his top priorities. Art was all-important to him. But he had to take on commercial gigs to support himself – and that was how Heather had met him – when he had worked on commission for Ad Art, the company that had employed her since her graduation from Richmond Art Institute. By that time, she had worked there for three years, and many of the regular clients were requesting her rather than any of the other staff artists to design their projects and supervise them to completion. She had fantasized about quitting her nine-to-five job to go freelance – but she hadn't had the guts to do it till after she fell in love with Mark Pearson. He had encouraged her, whetting her appetite for the freedom *he* seemed to enjoy, pumping her up with praise laced with talk about how her bosses didn't really appreciate her, and making her believe that with the proper faith in herself she could make it on her own.

Well, thanks to his encouragement, she had taken the

big chance and had pulled it off. In the world of commercial art she was a glittering success, but in the personal relationship that meant the most to her, she was a dismal failure.

She had failed by succeeding. Mark was ashamed of not keeping pace with her, and it was killing their marriage. They had dreamed of how grand it would be to make it to the top together, and now he was afraid she was leaving him behind. But *she* hadn't changed. She still didn't mind supporting his vastly superior art by grinding out her inferior form of it. She was glad to be able to be a hack for him, relieving him of the demeaning burden. If it ever occurred to her that maybe she was more talented than she gave herself credit for, she subdued the notion.

Truth was, she had never been all that proud of her artwork, maybe because it came so easily for her. She could always toss off quick, eye-catching designs, cartoons, and illustrations, from the time she was a teenager. Even though she made money with the stuff now, she knew it was often facile, imitative, expedient rather than creative. She could pick up on a fad, give it a twist or a flare, and make it seem bright and new. That was her special cleverness. People liked it. It helped sell their products. She was thankful she had a marketable skill. Not a big talent, but nevertheless a marketable skill.

Mark, on the other hand, had in her view a wild and raging talent. A talent so gigantically original that it had overwhelmed her when he had first shown her some of his paintings and sculptures. Sooner or later it was bound to start overwhelming hordes of more important people. If he didn't lose faith in himself.

To Heather, it was sad and ironic that he had given her the courage to exercise her piddling skills, only to allow himself to be robbed of the drive behind his more legitimate and flamboyant gifts. She felt guilty, almost as if she were directly to blame for the self-doubt that was destroying him. At the same time she could see how he could find it harder and harder to turn out remarkable creations that would languish in his attic studio on the intangible hope that one day they would be displayed grandly in one of the top galleries. In the last four or five weeks, he hadn't so much as started on any new concepts. His excuse was that his creative juices weren't flowing. He had lashed out at Heather when she tried to rouse him from his doldrums by blurting that she had to work every day, whether she felt like it or not. With angry scorn, he had informed her that ideas like *his* had to wait to be born, they couldn't just be turned on and off like tap water.

She had swallowed the insult.

But how much more could she take?

How long could Mark go on hurting? How much longer before tension turned to incompatibility, and thwarted desire became desire no longer felt?

How many times could he try to make love to her and fail, before he would cease loving and start hating the symbol of his failure?

9

By 2:30 all the marriage encounter couples had arrived except Vernon and Rose Hearn. Dr Anita Walsh was socializing on the veranda when Brenda Meachum called her to the phone. It was Rose. She was calling from a pay phone at a gas station. Her thoughtfulness in letting Anita know that she and her husband would be late was nullified by her bubbleheaded excuse – something about a hassle with her hairdresser. 'We're still a hundred miles away,' she whined, as if the world had conspired to put her in this torturous predicament. 'And we had to stop for gas. And Vernon says we can't possibly make it to Carson Manor much before six, even if we don't get lost.'

'Well, try to make it a bit before six, if you can, without driving dangerously,' Anita said. 'Supper will be served at six or thereabouts, and it'll be nice if you have time to settle in first and get to know the other guests.'

Hanging up the phone, Anita was annoyed, even though she had tried to sound amiable. The Hearns were always late for their appointments at her office in Richmond, so she might have expected them to be late for the marriage encounter as well. Both in their forties, they were as irresponsible as adolescents. Their fear of growing old had produced in them a failure to mature properly. They relentlessly tried to dress and act younger than their years, to the point of absurdity. Anita was trying to guide them subtly toward more self-awareness, but often it seemed like a losing battle. Shaking her head over the opaqueness of some of the people she had to deal with and try to help, Anita came back outside. No one was on the veranda. Charles, still in jodhpurs and riding boots, was leading the guests around the side of the house on the first stage of the little tour he liked to give after everyone got a chance to unwind. Catching up, Anita told him about the Hearns.

'Well,' he said, 'it's their money. If they want to waste it, it's up to them.'

'But then they'll go home complaining about how little they got out of it,' Anita said for everyone's benefit, particularly Mark Pearson's.

For some reason, Mark seemed more truculent now than when he had first arrived. Heather edged towards him and tried to hold his hand, but he pulled it away.

The other young couple in the group – Harvey and Andrea Warnak – weren't getting along so smashingly either. Andrea was sticking close to Charles, while Harvey was lagging behind everybody else as if he didn't belong. He and his wife were both in their mid-twenties. He was a computer technician and she was a history teacher. They were a nice average couple, basically content with their lives and their marital relationship up until two years ago. Then Andrea began having dizzy spells and blurry vision which turned out to be caused by a brain tumour. It wasn't malignant, but it was so large and so intertwined with vital synapses that her chances of recovering from surgery were said to be virtually nonexistent. But, miraculously, she beat the odds, survived with mental faculties and motor functions unimpaired, and went home to what should have been great joy – and wasn't. Harvey had made such a valiant effort to cope with his grief over his wife's expected death that emotionally he had already written her off. The fact that she didn't die, after he had 'overprepared' himself for bereavement, sent him into a complex form of shock complicated by underlying resentment over his own suffering and guilt over the resentment. The Warnaks both needed to learn to accept and deal with this strange syndrome in order to re-create their former level of affection and commitment.

This afternoon Anita thought she could sense something that Charles may have missed due to his closeness to the couple, since they were his patients, not hers, back in Richmond. It seemed that a degree of patient-to-therapist transference was occurring between Andrea and Charles. This was a common phenomenon: for a patient to become mildly infatuated with the person who was understanding and sympathizing with him or her on a fairly intimate, albeit professional, level. It wasn't always easy for the therapist to avoid, because the patient was usually in an emotionally susceptible state. Therapists who tried to thwart it by remaining aloof, putting too much distance between themselves and their patients, risked diminishing their ability to relate to them and help them.

As much as Anita understood the phenomenon and knew that it wasn't Charles's fault, she still had to suppress a twinge of jealousy at seeing a younger woman romantically inclined towards her husband. For her, this natural reaction was easily stifled, since she possessed the requisite knowledge, experience, and confidence in Charles's love and loyalty. But for Harvey Warnak it was quite a different matter. He was straggling along, alternating between casting forlorn looks at the ground and hateful looks at Charles's back.

Oblivious to the memtal daggers, Charles led everyone to the cook house – a red brick outbuilding where the meals for the plantation had been prepared in pre-Civil War times. Of course the tour was right up Andrea's alley, since she was a history teacher. With a gleam in her eye that wasn't entirely pedagogical, she touched Charles's arm and said in a voice full of vivacious enthusiasm, 'This is marvellous, Charles! Did your Uncle Horace supervise all of the restoration of Carson Manor, or did you have a hand in it, too?'

'It was Anita's Uncle Horace,' Charles said, stepping back from her. 'He left it to us about the way you see it. He was a remarkable man. Always said that ours was a decadent age. He was right, too. I think he'd have been happier living in the eighteenth century, or no later than the nineteenth. So would I, in a way.'

'Me, too,' said Andrea. 'Things were far less complicated back then.'

'Certain medical problems were far less treatable, too!' Harvey Warnak piped up from his place at the rear of the group. He must have been trying to drag Andrea from her flight into the past with Charles to her place in the present with him, by reminding her that if she had lived back then she would never have survived a brain tumour. But she only perceived the apparent cruelty in his comment, not the strategy, and she looked stunned and hurt before she recovered her composure and followed Charles into the cook house.

It dawned on Anita that jealousy over his wife's attraction to her psychiatrist might be a good thing for Harvey. Maybe it was one thing for him to surrender his spouse to fate, but still another to surrender her to a fellow human being.

Amused by this way of looking at it, Anita lingered outside the cook house to talk with Ben and Sophie Harris, who had not gone in yet since it would've been tight quarters if everyone had piled in all at once. The Harrises – a nice, chubby, white-haired grandma and grandpa type – had the mildest affliction of any of the couples at the marriage encounter. They still *liked* each other, but they were getting on each other's nerves now that Ben was retired from his job as an industrial engineer, and they were both at home all day long, in each other's hair. All their children were grown up, married, and living far away with children of their own. Ben and Sophie's empty house seemed too big for them and yet too small. Instead of finding new interests that they could share, they were always encroaching on each other's territory, nagging and fussing at each other. But one would never guess it by the way they were today – quite relaxed and amiable, which only went to prove that they needed to get outside themselves and find a bit of purpose to their lives, even if they had to manufacture it.

However, this perception aside, Anita could also see how having to contend with Ben Harris twenty-four hours a day could get to be a major annoyance. He was full of garrulous suggestions for 'improving' things – everything from the rain gutters on the manor house to the lighting arrangements in the guest rooms – never mind that his changes would do away with the antebellum flavour of the place. Apparently, even though he was a *retired* industrial engineer, he couldn't stop tinkering with people's habits and preferences, trying to improve their efficiency. This must be what Sophie had meant when she had complained in their first counselling session, several weeks ago, 'He's always telling me how to do my washing, my cooking, my ironing, or my cleaning. He doesn't have anybody to boss anymore except me, so now he wants to run my whole household, when I've been doing it myself quite satisfactorily for forty-three years. I could take a little of his meddling when he'd only do it after work and on weekends, but now he's on my back constantly, as if he doesn't have anything better to do with himself.'

Behind her husband's back, Sophie pursed her lips and shook her head disapprovingly as he delivered an enthusiastic discourse on how the stables could be partially converted to garage space, eliminating the need for a separate garage. Anita politely nodded and smiled, as if she and Charles would phone the wreckers and builders first thing in the morning. She was saved from the pantomime when Sanford and Joan Berman came out of the cook house and Sophie dragged Ben in with her.

The Bermans obviously weren't history buffs. They mumbled some cursory remarks about how 'interesting and quaint' it was to see the kinds of utensils and stoves used 'in olden times'. Then they took to admiring 'the beautiful horses' – Bullet and Lightning – as George Stone was leading them out of the corral so they could graze.

Like the Harrises and the Hearns, the Bermans were Anita's patients on a regular basis in Richmond. Sanford was also attending Alcoholics Anonymous. He hadn't had a drink for over a year, and he looked pretty healthy now – a big, fleshy, redheaded man, forty-one years old – who had been quite dissipated when he and Joan first sought counselling. She was a short, pudgy brunette – much more overweight than Anita. But she was a loving and dutiful wife, determined to stick with her husband so long as he continued to fight his alcohol addiction and work with her to improve their marriage.

When Charles ushered the other three couples out of the cook house, Harvey Warnak was making an effort to stay beside Andrea, but she was playing hard to get. Either she was captivated by Charles and what he had to say, or – this possibility occurred to Anita for the first time – she wanted Harvey to think so. It wouldn't be the first time that a woman excited a man's interest by pretending to prefer someone else. Anita liked that interpretation better than the transference theory. She could respect Andrea for trying to pull it off and could even root for her if she wasn't really trying to land Charles.

Charles was pointing at the tractor shed, telling everyone it was in the same place where the servants' quarters used to be.

'Don't you mean slave quarters?' Mark Pearson interjected.

'Well, what I mean is house servants,' Charles explained, 'as opposed to field hands. When slavery was going on, the house servants were slaves as were the field hands, but house servants had more privileges and were generally treated better. After the Civil War, the house servants and the field hands weren't technically slaves, of course – they were paid and were supposed to be free – but in reality their lot didn't improve much. Their freedom was mostly on paper. They couldn't be sold at auction – that was the one big difference.'

'How many slaves lived here?' Heather Pearson asked.

'Around three hundred at the peak,' said Charles. 'The Carson family owned the whole valley – over a hundred thousand acres. The main commercial crop was tobacco, for shipment to London. But like the other great southern plantations, Carson Manor was almost wholly self-sufficient. It grew its own food, and had its own icehouse, dairy, blacksmith shop, carpenter shop, and so on.'

'Must've been magnificent!' Ben Harris exclaimed, licking his lips at the thought of all the people and activities he could've supervised.

'Not so magnificent for the slaves,' said his wife Sophie.

Charles led the way behind the stables to the area where the old slave quarters for the field hands used to be. The outlines of some of the floor plans had been excavated and could be seen as rough rectangular patterns of old, crumbling brick. 'The bricks were made right here on the plantation out of native clay,' said Charles. 'One of the reasons for making the huts so sturdy in the early days of Virginia settlements was so they could withstand Indian attacks. They were like little blockhouse fortifications with strong doors and small, heavily shuttered windows. The reason for the excavation here is that Uncle Horace was intending to reconstruct one or two of the huts before he died. Anita and I hope to carry out the task one of these days.'

'That'd be fantastic,' said Andrea Warnak, gazing admiringly at Charles, and Charles alone, as if he hadn't even mentioned his wife as a partner in the plans.

'You know,' said Sanford Berman, 'you could turn this place into a real tourist grabber.' He sounded perky for the first time, now that he was considering how to convert historical value into monetary value. 'You already have the house done up with the right artifacts and all – but it's not enough, you know what I mean? There'd be more to it if you could set up the blacksmith shop, the slave quarters, the dairy and all – maybe with manikins dressed up like slaves and overseers. Then you could knock down a hefty admission price – call it Carson Olde Tyme Plantation, something like that.'

'That would be crass and ignorant!' Andrea Warnak blurted.

'Actually,' said Charles, more diplomatically, 'we really don't want to go public with it. Anita and I enjoy it too much just the way it is.'

On the way back from behind the stables, Anita stopped to talk with George Stone. 'Don't forget, George,' she reminded, 'you have to go into Carsonville for us this afternoon to pick up a big grocery order. Meredith has the list. You can get it from her before you leave.'

'Yes, ma'am,' said George. 'I'll be taking off in an hour or so, after I get the horses back in the corral. I told Sarah I'd be stopping off early for my supper. Anything else you and Doctor Chuck want me to do?'

'Nothing I can think of offhand. Why didn't Janie come today?'

'Her mama said she needed her to do some chores.'

Anita and George exchanged a look, signifying that

they both knew the chores were an excuse to keep Janie away.

Charles was passing out tablets and felt-tip pens to everybody as Anita mounted the wide stone steps to the veranda. He began explaining the first serious activity of the marriage encounter: letter writing. Everybody was to split up, and the individuals were to go to separate places on the grounds, where they each would be totally alone. Then, using this privacy for contemplation and reflection, each person was to write a letter to his or her spouse, revealing the most intimate thoughts and feelings about the marital relationship. 'You have to say all the things to your husband or wife that you're not saying now,' said Charles. 'All your desires, wants, and frustrations. The good and the bad. Tender moments and heartaches. Exactly what you think of the other person, and what you want from him or her that you're not getting now.'

'Don't be afraid to reveal yourself,' said Anita. 'These letters are an excellent device for clarifying your thoughts and feelings and making you see things in a new light.'

'What happens to the letters when we're done?' Heather Pearson asked with some trepidation.

'You're each going to keep your own,' said Anita. 'Don't worry, we're not going to collect them. Nobody will ever read your letter but yourself, unless you give it to somebody. We promise you that in advance, so you'll be motivated to put your honest effort into it.'

What Anita had told them all was partially a trick. Later in the marriage encounter, the husbands and wives were going to be given the opportunity to exchange the letters and reveal themselves to each other in a way they had never done before.

10

At three o'clock that Thursday afternoon, Jim Spencer was working on a last-ditch idea of how to stop the Green Brigade from ever getting to Cuba. As he talked on the phone or anxiously waited for callbacks from important people, he watched a portable colour television that had been set up on the prescription counter of the drugstore.

What he was seeing turned his stomach. It was a sorry day for America when a murderous communist punk like Wilson Woodruff could go on network TV to give 'an address to the nation'.

Inside the Manhattan National Bank, a camera panned the gloating faces of a contingent of terrorists who had their guns trained on six of the twelve remaining hostages. Spencer had been told by Colonel Mao that the other six hostages would be held in a separate room behind a locked door with guns at their throats, so they would be sure to die if Spencer tried any kind of trick – like sending in SWAT men disguised as part of the television crew.

The panning camera stopped and zoomed back to reveal General Kintay in full Green Brigade regalia, including a gold serpent on his beret and a chest full of self-bestowed medals. In his green fatigues, he was tall, narrow-shouldered, light-skinned. His facial features were more Caucasian then Negroid. Spencer had grudgingly to admit that Kintay had a certain evil charisma, a commanding presence. No doubt the lunatic zeal in his coal-black eyes and the subtly sensuous, sadistic sneer on his lips helped him attract his special type of followers.

Kintay was standing behind a podium, flanked by his mistress Colonel Mao and his main sidekick from Attica, a skinny little white weirdo with a mean, sneaky look, whose *nom de guerre* was 'Colonel Chu'. The backdrop for the sinister trio was the wall-mounted flag of the Green Brigade: a parody of the United States flag consisting of thirteen green and white stripes with a coiled green serpent on a white field.

To Jim Spencer's disgust, the voice-over television commentator introduced the three terrorist leaders with respect and even awe, as if they were high-ranking officers of an army of foreign conquerors. Then Kintay began to speak in a voice that was curiously high-pitched and soft, almost effeminate, belying the violence that he advocated – or making it more palatable.

'Greetings,' said Kintay. 'Greetings of profound love to the oppressed masses, to all comrades in arms, and to all comrades in the concentration camps of fascist America. I am General Kintay. I speak to you in memory of Cinque, Fahizah, Gabi, Zoya, Kojo, and Gelina. I speak to unite all believers in the Symbionese Liberation Army, the New World Liberation Front, the Black Liberation Army, and *all other* elements of the glorious people's struggle against the United States Empire. Whatever you call yourselves, whatever banner you fight under, you are *all* spiritual soldiers of the Green Brigade!'

At this, both Colonel Mao and Colonel Chu shot their arms out in a clenched-fist salute. 'Comrades, we salute you!' they shouted in unison.

Jim Spencer angrily extended his middle finger at the television screen. The phone rang and he whirled to pick it up. It was FBI headquarters in Washington. He was put on hold for the director. He tried to formulate his idea in his own mind with conciseness and clarity, so he could present it in its best light. He couldn't stand the thought of not being allowed to try *something* that might wipe out the madness that Kintay was puking out on the TV into every naïve, susceptible mind in America.

'The ruling class and all its pig agents cannot destroy us if we join together,' Kintay said. 'They cannot continue to exploit, murder, and imprison an undivided army of the people. Today we have proved that the FBI and the CIA and the other fascist dogs are not invincible. Today we have won a battle, but the war is still ahead of us. The armed might of the pigs is terrible, and their capacity for brutality and oppression is infinite, because they wish to keep us in slavery forever. But we must remember the words of our dear comrade Ho Chi Minh: Today the locust fights the elephant, but tomorrow the elephant will be disembowelled!'

The director of the FBI came on the line, and Jim Spancer began explaining his idea and why he believed it could work. He made it clear that he had already talked to certain experts and key people and had enlisted their approval and cooperation. Intent on his presentation, Spencer barely heard Kintay as he launched into the wrap-up of his speech.

'The pigs think we are suicidal fools because we resist them by taking up arms. I say to them that like our slain SLA brethren we will die, if necessary, in a just cause. We will bring about the greening of America, even if we ourselves do not live to see it.'

Spencer's half-attuned ear caught the part about being willing to die. If the director approved his plan, he might be able to fulfil that willingness for Kintay and his gang.

'Power to the people! Power to the people!' Mao and Chu chanted before Kintay went on.

'Our past as loyal, poor, or middle-class Americans was meaningless, full of wasted potential and desperate pessimism, because we sensed the emptiness of capitalist America even before we could understand it. But now our eyes are opened on the future. Today we leave for Cuba and a rendezvous of destiny with our great and wise comrade, Fidel Castro. From Cuba, we will train all

71

who come to join us – all who want to learn to be freedom fighters like ourselves. We will recruit and arm and increase the power of the Green Brigade, looking forward to the final invasion and destruction of the United States Empire. We will live for the day when our spark will have ignited a great fire. In the flames of freedom, the pigs will burn. Their oppression will melt to smoke, and their evil spirit will turn to ashes!'

Kintay, Mao, and Chu all clenched their fists. In fanatical unison they shouted, 'Death to the beast of fascism that feasts on the sould of the people!'

Sensing by the kinds of questions he was being asked that his ideas were making a favourable impression on the FBI director, Jim Spencer again gave the middle finger to the television set.

11

Dr Charles Walsh was late joining his guests for supper because he gave in to his compulsion to watch the six o'clock news.

He found out that roughly an hour ago, at 5:09 P.M., a Boeing 747 had left LaGuardia, carrying the Green Brigade and their hostages. There was a clip of the plane taking off. Then there was some shots of General Kintay delivering his televised speech.

Charles wanted to hear Kintay expounding his philosophy, however half-baked it might be, for the sake of the insights it might provide into the mind of a sociopath. But nothing was shown lip-sync; instead the TV commentator went voice-over, rehashing the biographical profile of Kintay that Charles had heard on the noon news. Then, to a reprise of graphic footage of police barricades, deployed SWAT specialists, and dead or dying hostages, the commentator began capsulizing the horrendous events that had unfolded since the takeover of the Manhattan National Bank yesterday afternoon.

Thanks to the magic of television, Charles told himself with wry sarcasm, all manner of blood and gore and insanity could be brought into the home. His sensibilities could be assaulted and his appetite ruined while he was putting on his dinner jacket and knotting his tie.

It was his own fault. He had allowed the intrusion by pushing the button, lighting up the tube. He was still edgy. Still couldn't shake the images of last night's nightmare. Something told him that he might not rest easy unless he watched this evening's news to make sure that the plane full of terrorists had passed over Virginia and was gone.

12

While the Green Brigade was in a commandeered Boeing 747 heading towards Cuba, Jim Spencer was on his way to Charlottesville, Virginia, in a FBI LearJet. His SWAT team commandos were flying with him – forty heavily armed, handpicked men, thoroughly trained in guerrilla combat and counter-insurgency.

With the approval of the FBI director, Spencer had put into motion his clever but risky plan for preventing the terrorists from getting out of the United States. The director had told him, 'This is your baby all the way, Jim. You'll be on your own hook, logistical details and all. If anything goes wrong, you must assume full responsibility. Whatever happens, the Bureau must not be embarrassed.' Spencer had accepted those conditions. He was itching for a rendezous in Charlottesville with Kintay and his gang of punk fanatics.

The pilot and copilot of the 747, Larry Warner and Dave Rice, were both FBI agents masquerading as airline employees. Rice was doubling as flight navigator so he and Warner could go it alone. A full crew wouldn't be lost – just two men – if something went wrong and the terrorists turned on them. Warner and Rice had volunteered for this assignment after Jim Spencer's plan had been explained to them. They knew how the plane was rigged and they understood what they had to do.

The emergency oxygen supply to the passenger area of the jetliner was not functioning; on Spencer's orders it had been turned off by the maintenance crew. The only oxygen masks with oxygen truly available were those serving Warner and Rice. The plan was for them to take the plane up to an excessively high altitude – about 80,000 feet – where the atmosphere would be so thin that everyone aboard would start gasping for air. All would don masks when Warner and Rice created the artificial emergency, but the cockpit alone would be supplied with oxygen, and only the pilot's and copilot's seats, so that the passengers – hostages and terrorists alike – would succumb to anoxia and pass out. When they woke up they would find themselves breathing comfortably, at a lower altitude, and Dave Rice would be guarding them with one of the machine guns taken out of their hands while they were unconscious. Then the plane could be landed in Charlottesville – at a small, predesignated, cordoned-off airport – where Spencer and his SWAT commandos would be waiting to take the terrorists into custody.

He almost hoped that Kintay would provoke a shoot-out. It would be more satisfying to see the enemies of society blasted to bits and burned to ashes, like the SLA in Los Angeles, than to see them put behind bars for a few years, killing time and dreaming of going back to killing loyal citizens.

The two hostages already 'executed' by Colonel Mao had been loan officers of the Manhattan National Bank. This had made them 'capitalist pigs' in her eyes; the 'crime of usury' had condemned them to death. Both had been married men with young children to raise. Now they wouldn't be around for the children to grow up and turn against them, as children nowadays were so prone to do to their parents, after the parents slaved and sacrificed to give them the best of everything.

Ruefully, Spencer thought of his daughter Caroline and dreaded to imagine what sort of trouble she'd be getting into tonight. Before leaving New York, he had phoned her to let her know he wouldn't be coming home. He had counted thirteen rings before she finally answered.

He should've hung up, but he hadn't done so and didn't know why. To him it was unnatural, insipid, even perverse, that a man's daughter could sleep so soundly – in late afternoon – while knowing his life may be on the line. Didn't she realize the danger? Did she block it out so she wouldn't have to deal with it? Or did she simply not give a damn? Maybe it was his fault for shielding her from worries and trauma all through her growing-up years. Untouched by any of life's uglier realities, she now seemed half deadened to any realities at all, whether ugly or beautiful. She had to take drugs to 'get her head in a groovy place' – in other words, to be able to feel.

When Spencer had talked with Caroline on the phone, all he had heard in her voice was a bitchy crankiness because her sleep had been disturbed. She hadn't even asked him to be careful. 'I love you, Daddy' would have been too much to hope for.

Spencer wondered if maybe his wife had lived, instead of dying of cancer eight years ago, their daughter mightn't have turned out so spoilt. Or, maybe things would've been better if he had got married again to a good woman. Who could tell what sort of magic might have worked? Where was the key to success in raising children? How could there be any foolproof formula in a sick, decadent society that was corrupting and poisoning its youth with drugs, sex, and violence?

Lighting still another cigarette from the butt of his previous one, Jim Spencer grimaced, recalling how, when he had tried to talk to Caroline about the hazards of marijuana, she had sassed him, saying, '*You* use drugs too, but they're socially acceptable ones – alcohol and nicotine.' And when he had broached the subject of sex with love and commitment versus meaningless promiscuity, she had sneered, 'Just because you've stayed celibate since Mommy died, it doesn't mean everybody else has to!' He had slapped her face then, and they hadn't spoken to one another for three weeks afterwards. He had tried to make himself believe that he didn't care about her anymore. He could take her insolence about his three-pack-a-day cigarette habit and his need for three or four martinis to help him unwind each evening, but he couldn't handle her flippancy about her dead mother and his lack of desire for any other woman.

What had kept Spencer going after his wife died was his drive to make America a better place for his daughter to grow up in. Now he was stunned and bitter over the realization that Caroline had contempt for his mission. He knew that she saw him as an obsessive-complusive tyrant, trying to order and regiment all of society the way he had tried to order and regiment her private life. She was determined to prove that he didn't have control over her any longer, by showing him that she could wreck her own mind and body if she so chose. No way could he stop her from making 'scorched earth' of herself, no matter how much it made him bleed.

He could almost wish that she would turn her neurosis outwards, like the terrorists of the Green Brigade. Maybe then she would hate what he stood for, instead of staunchly and incorrigibly hating only him.

13

Larry Warner and Dave Rice had their doubts about pulling off Jim Spencer's little gambit. As they handled the controls of the Boeing 747, they were being guarded by two terrorists – Mickey Holtz and Janet Fagan – who knew how to read compasses and gauges and plot flight coordinates. When the airplane had lifted off the ground at LaGuardia, they had kissed each other and talked excitedly of their plan to get married in Cuba. Except for being heavily armed, they looked like a nice average couple. They weren't wearing camouflage fatigues – just denim jeans and grey cotton workshirts – the uniform of the proletariat.

Larry Warner was thirty-eight years old, and Dave Rice was thirty-six. Both were shrewd, intelligent, and in excellent physical condition. Warner was stocky without being fat, his face was large and square, his dark brown hair was greying at the temples. Because Rice was blond, fine-boned, and boyishly handsome, he had looked ten years younger than Warner till they both took off their officers' caps revealing that Rice was completely bald on top. They were both former Air Force men with numerous bombing missions over Vietnam and Laos under their belts. Warner had tried commercial aviation for a while but had found it all too dull. Rice had been recruited by the FBI before his Air Force enlistment was up. Before volunteering to fly (and abort) the Green Brigade flight to Cuba, they had been on loan to the CIA for some secret bombing raids against the Sandinistas in Central America. There was little doubt in their minds that if General Kintay or any of his honchos found out about their military records, they wouldn't be allowed to live too long after their usefulness to the terrorists had been expended.

For that matter, there was no guarantee that Kintay, Mao, and Chu didn't intend to execute the hostages and the pilots once they had landed in Havana. Warner and Rice would put nothing past the lunatics with the guns. So they knew that they had to try taking the 747 up into rarefied air, even though Fagan and Holtz might catch on. Some way had to be found to divert their attention from the altimeter.

Not counting the pilot and copilot, there were twelve hostages and forty-three terrorists aboard the plane. General Kintay, Colonel Mao, and Colonel Chu were sitting three abreast in the first-class section, in the first row of seats. Behind them were the rest of their soldiers, except for two who were guarding the hostages back in the coach section. All had their seatbelts buckled in case the pilot tried something or in case the aircraft was attacked. Kintay had warned his people that the 'enemies of the people' might decide to shoot the plane from the skies, then come up with some trumped-up story as to why it had gone down so the general public wouldn't complain too much about the hostages being sacrificed.

In the coach section, eleven of the hostages were sitting close together, while one was two rows apart from the rest. Her name was Elizabeth Stoddard, and she was a beautiful and normally arrogant young woman, used to being in cool, haughty control over her own destiny, and totally unaccustomed to dreading what others might do to her. At twenty-nine, she had been married and divorced twice, increasing her wealth by each transaction, and at the moment she was married to the board chairman of a Fortune 500 corporation. Back at the Manhattan National Bank, the terrorists had viewed the computer printouts on her various accounts and had made her unlock her safety deposit box, so they knew everything about her insofar as money and status were concerned. This was one time in her life that her credentials did not bode well for her. She was the kind of 'exploiter of the masses' that the Green Brigade loved to hate.

Mortally afraid of the terrible predicament she was in, she had tried to sway Colonel Chu while he was interrogating her. She had pointed out the advantage of keeping her for ransom rather than choosing her as one of the hostages to be executed. Trying to demonstrate a kinship with the proletariat, she had spoken of the many charities that she and her husband helped support. But Colonel Chu had laughed in her face as he reached out and ripped her blouse open. Tearfully and desperately giving in to him, she had forced herself to stand still while he fondled her breasts. Then she had tremblingly helped him undress her. 'Please,' she had whispered meekly. 'Please make the others leave.' A half sneer had crossed his lips as he stared at her nakedness. But he ordered the two armed guards to go out of the bank president's office and shut the door. During the next couple of hours – between the arrival of the helicopter from Attica and the setting up of the TV broadcast – she had tried to please Colonel Chu more than she had ever pleased any other man. At first he was too ravenous to appreciate her skills. Sexually pent-up and deprived through a long prison term, once he was inside her there was no way of holding him back. But after his first orgasm, he wanted many more . . . and she was able to relax him and do everything for him that she wanted and needed to do. She needed to bond herself to him – a bond of sex and cruelty that would make him reluctant to let her go.

Now, on the plane, her dire hope was that as long as Chu's animal appetites weren't satiated, he would keep her alive. She would be one of his favourites. In fact, she wanted to believe that she had been singled out for special dispensation by being placed apart from the other hostages when they had been herded into their seats.

The captives were all sitting in an eerie, unnatural quiet, scared to make any move or sound that might draw the attention of their guards. Some were silently praying. Despite the promise of being released in Havana, many doubted that they would ever see their friends and families again. They were horrifyingly aware that each second of flight time was bringing them closer to a final determination of their fate.

The two guards – Green Brigade guerrillas in tee shirts and faded jeans – were turned sideways in the opposite section of seats, seven rows apart so they could cover all the hostages in a crossfire with their submachine guns. They were also armed with .45 automatics in green canvas holsters, and their gunbelts were hung with cartridges, ammo clips, and grenades. They looked frightfully tired and edgy. They had been awake all night under constant pressure from the police and the FBI. It was the kind of strain that produced bloodshot, puffy eyes and itchy trigger fingers.

Elizabeth Stoddard ran her tongue over her lips, barely mustering enough saliva to moisten them. Always distrustful of people beneath her own station, she couldn't stop worrying that some hostage other than herself might do something that would bring her to grief. She sat rigidly, not daring to turn her head and look over her shoulder or anywhere else except straight ahead. She had herself braced to remain on her best behaviour. She fervently wished to be excluded from the guards' crossfire if somebody else's foolish move provoked it.

The blue curtain parted at the head of the centre aisle, and all the hostages held their breath as Colonel Chu strode through. With a snake on his armband and a gold eagle on his beret, the skinny little man in camouflage fatigues had the strut and sneer of a victim turned into a victimizer.

Elizabeth Stoddard looked up, seductively smiling at him as he swaggered down the aisle. She had tried her best to please him sexually a few hours ago. She tried to believe that there was no reason why he should not like her now, at least a little, because after all, men far more wealthy and powerful than Chu had fallen madly in love with her.

He stopped alongside her row of seats. Then he unholstered his Luger. 'Come with me, Elizabeth,' he said in a soft but commanding tone.

Her mouth went dry. Her chin trembled and her smile deserted her. When she tried to stand, her knees were too weak and she fell back. She pulled herself up by holding on to the back of the seat in front of her.

'Don't be afraid,' he said with an odd, jarring gentleness. 'We decided we need a hostage in the cockpit, in case the pilots try something funny.'

Shakily she moved ahead of Chu up the aisle, his pistol jabbing her hard in the spine when she stumbled backwards on her rubbery legs. She wanted to think she was still safe. She told herself it made sense: a hostage in the cockpit. But she knew that people going to the gas chambers had thought it made sense when the Nazis told them they were going to take showers.

Chu prodded Elizabeth through the first-class compartment, past rows of Green Brigade brigands – some of whom were chatting in low whispers, some playing cards using seat trays as tables, and some sleeping in fitful exhaustion. When Elizabeth came by General Kintay and Colonel Mao, they did not look up at her. Were they ignoring her because she was condemned? Perhaps for them she did not exist any longer, the sentence having already been passed. In spite of the gun in her ribs, she turned to face them. She tried to speak boldly but her voice came out in a dry, hoarse whisper. 'My husband will pay millions for me. You would be wiser to select somebody else. What good will I be to you if I'm dead?'

Kintay looked at her then, and chuckled wryly.

'How will your husband know?' Mao jeered. 'If we tell him you're still alive?'

Colonel Chu shoved her forward through the open door of the cockpit. Her despair was bottomless now because at last she realized that none of her attributes would save her. Not beauty nor sex nor money would save her from whatever her captors wanted to do.

Her eyes blurring with tears, she grasped the presence of the pilot and copilot, the myriad of controls and instruments, the terrorist guards – Fagan and Holtz – and the vista of blue sky and puffy white clouds that she might never see again from the earth, looking skyward. She sank to her knees and hugged Chu's legs, pleading, 'Save me . . . please . . . save me.' She sobbed, 'I'll do anything you ask . . . I'll be your woman.'

'You gotta understand,' Chu said with a faint trace of sympathy. 'You're a fine piece of ass, baby, but hardly a sister of the revolution.' He raised his pistol and brought it down hard, like a hammer, across the top of her head, clubbing her unconscious.

Larry Warner and Dave Rice watched all this with outward stoicism, while inwardly they were tensed, waiting for some confusion to erupt that they might take advantage of. If the terrorists – especially Fagan and Holtz – could be distracted, they might not notice if the plane started climbing to higher altitude.

General Kintay came into the cockpit. He looked at the woman who was lying face downward at Colonel Chu's feet, her blonde hair matted with blood where he had bludgeoned her.

Eyeing Warner and Rice, Kintay said, 'We have no

compunction against sentencing our enemies to death. But perhaps you doubt this.'

'We don't doubt it at all,' said Warner. 'We know you killed two hostages at the bank.'

'But maybe you think the plane is a different story.'

'Why should it be?' said Warner. 'But no further killing is necessary. I promise you, this very day you'll step on to Cuban soil.'

'Your word means nothing to me,' Kintay sneered. 'I think you need to see with your own eyes what will happen if you give us the slightest suspicion that you may betray our cause by not keeping this plane on its proper course.'

'Fagan and Holtz can read the instruments,' said Warner. 'Can't they? Or aren't you confident of their expertise?'

'Instruments can be tampered with,' Kintay countered. He nodded to Chu, who stooped to point his pistol at the base of Elizabeth Stoddard's skull.

'No! Don't!' Dave Rice exclaimed. 'If you miss, you'll blow a hole in the fuselage – the cabin will depressurize!'

But Chu pulled the trigger. The blast echoed in the confinement of the cockpit, and the unconscious woman's head exploded like a shattered melon. Chu leapt back to avoid the splatter.

'One hostage will be executed each time you give us cause to question your obedience,' Kintay warned Warner and Rice. Then he and Chu went back to the first-class compartment.

Warner stole a glance at Fagan and Holtz, who were standing by the rearward instrument panel. The terrorist couple looked badly shaken; their faces were ashen. They were obviously strangers to violence, and probably had never fundamentally realized that their escapade would cause people to die. Now they were seeing ugly death up close. They were dazed, dumbfounded, trying to act tough while their guts were turning to water. Their resolve was turning to mush.

In such a state, would they remember to check the altimeter occasionally? Kintay himself had emphasized the urgency of keeping the plane on course for Cuba. On course but not *low*. The terrorists were mainly concerned with direction and speed. They wanted to be sure they were headed south, fast. Hopefully, they wouldn't be likely to notice if the course was diverted *upward*.

Warner decided that he would take the chance as soon as he got in range of Charlottesville, Virginia.

14

Supper at Carson Manor was an old-time Southern feast. Anita went off her diet to enjoy it. Charles loved the feeling of playing host in a style that exemplified traditional plantation hospitality.

The dining room, which in antebellum times had also served as a music hall and dancing hall, was extraordinarily spacious and elegant. There were large fireplaces at either end of the long room, decorated with carved Italian tile and marble. On the mantel and sideboards were porcelain figurines of colonial ladies and gentlemen and ornate vases of dried flowers. On the pale green walls, above the darker green wainscoting, silver sconces were symmetrically spaced between oil paintings of eighteenth-century equestrian and pastoral scenes.

The table service was composed of antique china, pewter, and crystal of delicate craftsmanship. The main courses were roast pheasant with oyster stuffing, baked Virginia ham, and lemon-broiled Potomac shad. There were numerous side dishes and garnishes including buttered parsnips, turnips, sweet potatoes, hot hash, and Indian pudding. Dessert was Charleston syllabub made of cream, Rhine wine, strong dry sack, lemon juice, and sugar.

During the course of the meal, Charles pointed out that all the dishes had been prepared according to authentic pre-Civil War recipes. They were served proudly by Brenda and Meredith Meachum, who received a toast and a round of applause for their efforts.

Andrea Warnak, who had contrived to sit to the left of Charles Walsh while Anita sat to his right, bubbled and gushed over everything. When she fell silent for an unusually long time, it was obviously so she could think of how to phrase something impressive to say. While everyone was having coffee and syllabub, she remarked that she could almost feel ghosts in this room. She could picture the oriental carpet and the long dining table rolled aside so that Confederate officers and their ladies in crinoline dresses could waltz beneath the crystal chandelier to the haunting music of violins and harpsichords.

She looked to Charles for approval after uttering this mouthful. Everyone else was numbed to silence. So was Charles, it turned out. The first person to pipe up was Sanford Berman, who said, 'Boy, you can sure tell you're a history teacher!'

'What's wrong with history teachers?' Andrea demanded, her green eyes flashing.

'Their minds aren't on reality,' said Sanford. 'Always living in the past. Making everybody else memorize dates and facts about stuff that's long gone.'

At that, Charles found his voice. 'The past is not only not dead, it is not even past. I forget who said that, but it's very true.'

'But what in the heck does it mean?' Sanford Berman blurted, as if it couldn't possibly mean anything that made much sense.

'Well, try to snip it off,' said Andrea, thrilled at having Charles as her ally. 'Where would you use the scissors? If the past is past, when did it end?'

'The Roman Empire ended,' Berman squelched. 'It's over and done with.'

'It most surely isn't,' Andrea snapped, becoming progressively angrier. 'We still have Roman laws, customs, and languages – even Roman roads and aqueducts. The world is still being affected by everything that happened back then.'

'But why study about it?' said Sanford Berman. 'Why

memorize a bunch of stupid dates? I *hated* history when I was in school.'

'If all you got out of it was memorizing dates, I hardly blame you,' said Charles. 'History should be studied for the intellectual and emotional insights it provides. Time is a continuum. Any man – or nation – that doesn't comprehend the past is like an individual with amnesia. We have to learn where we've been so we can have some idea where we're going.'

'Exactly!' Andrea pounced. 'I never make my eighth graders memorize dates. I want them to understand the flow of events and how man shapes his own destiny.'

'That's what makes you a good teacher, honey,' said Harvey Warnak, putting his hand on his wife's arm.

But she ignored Harvey's attempt to ingratiate himself, as if she hadn't felt his touch. Looking at no one else but Charles, she said, 'Thanks for sticking up for me. I admire the way you express yourself. You're a very charming and perceptive man.'

'I guess that implies I'm not,' said Sanford Berman in a blustery but petulant tone. 'Well, I'll be the first to admit I'm no egghead. I like living in the twentieth century. You can talk and talk about ancient history, but to me it's still pretty dry stuff – unless you can make a buck out of it, like I was saying earlier, out by the slave cabins.'

'Maybe each cabin could have its own coin-operated turnstile,' Andrea Warnak quipped indignantly. 'How would you like *that*, Anita?'

The question took Anita Walsh by surprise. She hadn't expected Andrea to address any clever remarks to her rather than to Charles. Besides, she had been only half listening to the argumentative conversation. 'I'm sorry,' she said. 'I'm afraid my mind was wandering. My eyes were on the two empty place-settings for Vernon and Rose Hearn. I can't understand why they haven't shown up yet. I hope they haven't had an accident.'

'I doubt it,' said Charles. 'Aren't they the ones who are always late?'

'Yes, but not *this* late. I'm getting worried.'

'Let's adjourn to the parlour for an after-dinner sherry,' Charles suggested. 'Probably by the time we get it poured, the Hearns will arrive.'

15

On board the commandeered 747, one of the hostages –
a small, pale, baldheaded man with a bony face, thick lips,
and thick eyeglasses – wasn't thinking only of whether or
not his life would be spared if the plane landed in Havana.
He was thinking about the money in the hands of the
terrorists. Two million dollars. It was more than enough
cash for a man to start a new life and to live however he
wished.

Fred Coogan was a theatre projectionist, bitterly dis-
satisfied with the station to which society had relegated
him. He had entered the Manhattan National Bank
yesterday afternoon to deposit his meagre paycheque. A
morose, socially withdrawn bachelor, who at age thirty-
seven still lived with his domineering, hypochondriacal
mother, Fred worked in a decrepit movie house on 42nd
Street where the usual fare was pornography or martial
arts films dawn to dusk. His big self-indulgences were his
weapons collection, his firing-range practice, and his
karate lessons – all berated by his mother as a sick, stupid
waste of money. She didn't understand that civil war was
coming to America – but Fred knew it with all his heart
and he didn't need the Green Brigade to prove it to
him. For the past six years he had been avidly reading
survivalist books and magazines, learning how to defend
himself, and stocking up – to the extent he could afford
to do so – on the kinds of equipment and food supplies
that would become absolutely necessary when there was
a complete breakdown of law and order. All his mother
did was complain about how the stuff messed up the
spare room.

She begrudged him the spare room, for God's sake, when in his daydreams he wanted to own a fortress, a private domain in rugged, barely accessible terrain, secured by artillery and land mines and an electrified fence. But only the wealthy could afford to be properly protected. Fred Coogan could scrimp and save all he wanted, and he'd be lucky to survive the shoot-out in Manhattan.

But now, on this plane was the means to his salvation. Two million dollars. Kintay and his band were guarding sacks full of greenbacks, in the first-class compartment.

When Fred came out of the house each day, he always carried some type of secret weapon to give himself a sense of safety and power. Sometimes it might be a stiletto strapped to his calf; other times a flat, small-calibre automatic pistol in a thin holster clipped under his belt in the hollow of his spine. By sheer luck, he hadn't employed either of these two rather obvious devices yesterday morning, or else when the terrorists had searched him they would have stripped him of his weapon – although he looked so harmless that they hadn't really frisked him properly. If he had been wearing boots, they might have checked for a boot knife, but they hadn't bothered making him take off his shoes. Even if they had done so, they probably still would have failed to notice that the right shoe had a detachable heel that doubled as the butt of a short but excruciatingly sharp knife, called an Urban Slasher, whose narrow blade was concealed within the shoe's thick leather sole.

For Fred Coogan, being on this captured plane with a gang of terrorists, two million dollars in stolen money, and a secret weapon in his shoe was a dire challenge as well as an unreal opportunity. He felt as if the fates were testing the strength of his convictions, daring him to prove he had the guts to depend on his survival training and to seize this chance to set himself up properly in the embattled society he envisioned, where he could be one of the winners instead of the loser everybody thought he was now. He could leave his mother to fend for herself. Let her sink or swim without him if she was so smart.

But the only way he could figure out that he might pull it off was if he could get the knife at the throat of one of the terrorist leaders – Mao, Chu, or – preferably – Kintay. Then he could command obedience from the rest of the pack. He could force them to let the plane land, dropping him off and the money. Then he'd let it take off again. The Green Brigade could go to Cuba. He wouldn't give a damn, as long as he got his hands on the two million dollars.

When Colonel Chu had come into the coach to get Elizabeth Stoddard, he hadn't got down the aisle far enough for Fred Coogan to jump him, since Elizabeth had been sitting apart from the other hostages. As far as Coogan was concerned, she was a slut who had deserved to die. He had heard the loud crack of Chu's Luger, even above the droning of the plane's engines. The other hostages had immediately started gasping, sobbing, and praying, and Coogan had slumped and shuddered and covered his face with his hands – putting on a good act so the guards wouldn't think he was any less craven than the rest of the people they held captive. But he was just waiting and hoping for his opportunity. His mind was made up. If any of the Green Brigade honchos got close enough to him, he was going to strike.

The 747 was only an hour away from Charlottesville. Larry Warner and Dave Rice exchanged tense glances out of the corners of their eyes.

Elizabeth Stoddard's blood-caked body was still on the cockpit floor. Fagan and Holtz, the two squeamish terrorist guards, were sitting diagonally behind the pilot and copilot, trying to maintain tough poses with their Uzi submachine guns. They were tired, jumpy, and scared. Occasionally they would check the flight instruments to make sure the plane was on a direct course for Cuba. But they didn't pay much attention to the altimeter. And they kept their eyes averted from the dead body – obviously they didn't have the stomach to look at it.

Playing upon their queasiness, Dave Rice said, 'Can't we get somebody to drag the poor dead woman out of here? Or at least cover her up with something?'

Mickey Holtz pretended to sneer at the request, as if the corpse really didn't bother him. Then, with studied nonchalance, he said to his girlfriend, 'Janet, why don't you ask Colonel Chu if we can exchange the dead woman for another live hostage? It won't do us much good to shoot the pilot and copilot if they cross us. It would be better to have a third party's life at stake in here.'

'Good idea,' said Janet Fagan in a hard, brittle tone, trying to act like a tough gun moll. She jabbed the intercom button and her voice was broadcast over the entire plane, as she put her request in to Colonel Chu.

Rice and Warner had been hoping that she might be so anxious to get away from the corpse that she'd leave the cockpit to talk to her commander. But apparently she was scared of what might happen to her if she left her post without orders to do so.

Chu came into the cockpit, his Luger drawn in case he was stepping into some kind of trick. A sadistic gleam in his eyes, he said, 'Your suggestion is well taken. Another live hostage. I'll personally make the selection. And I'll ask two of our comrades to drag Elizabeth back to the coach section so she can be an example of what could happen to the other hostages if any of them are thinking of not behaving themselves.'

'Thank you, Colonel,' said Mickey Holtz. And Chu left to perform his enjoyable mission.

Opting for the risk that getting rid of the dead woman

and selecting another hostage would be a sufficient diversion, Larry Warner started to sneak the plane into a gradual climb towards an oxygen-poor altitude.

When Fred Coogan saw Colonel Chu coming into the coach section brandishing his Luger, he was already prepared to make his move. After hearing what was up over the intercom, he had crossed his legs, resting his right ankle on his left knee, and had surreptitiously removed the Urban Slasher built into the detachable heel of his right shoe. He was now concealing the knife in his right hand, the butt in his palm, the blade snug against his wrist.

Chu swaggered down the aisle, flicking his beady-eyed stare over the faces of the hostages, playing cat and mouse with them, keeping them in suspense over which one would be chosen. He chuckled derisively at Fred Coogan, who was cowering in his seat looking meek and trembly. Then, when Chu's gaze meandered elsewhere, Fred pounced, springing out of his seat, seizing Chu's wrist in a karate hold and making him drop the Luger as his arm was twisted behind his back in a half-nelson with the Urban Slasher against his throat 'Freeze!' Coogan yelled at the two guards. 'Or I'll slice your Colonel like a slaughtered pig!' Keeping the advantage of surprise working for himself, Coogan yanked the helpless Chu towards one of the perplexed, indecisive guards, made a grab at the guard's ammo belt, and ripped loose a grenade. 'Everybody do what I say! If you don't, I'll pull the pin and blow Colonel Chu to smithereens!'

Still holding the knife, Coogan kept Chu in a kind of bearhug as he dropped his hands to the colonel's belly and looped a finger through the pull-ring of the grenade.

'Kill him anyway!' Chu screamed. 'I order you to kill him!'

Coogan hadn't anticipated this willingness on the part

94

of the terrorist leader to be sacrificed, and he froze in a moment of self doubt. At that instant, Chu flexed his right knee, driving a hard backwards kick up between Coogan's legs. The sharp knife ripped open Chu's belly as he spun sideways, lashing out with his combat boot. Screaming in agony, Coogan dropped the knife and the grenade – but he had managed to pull the pin. As he sank to his knees, one of the guards smashed him in the face with the butt of a submachine gun. Chu kicked the grenade as hard as he could, and it went flying, bouncing and rolling under one of the seats halfway up the aisle. Bleeding from his ripped-open belly, Chu snatched a submachine gun from a guard's hands and riddled Coogan with bullets. At the same time, the grenade exploded with a deafening roar.

Because the grenade had rolled under the seats, the passengers were spared the mutilating effects of hot shrapnel. But the force of the blast had been concentrated in such a way that the damage to the 747 was maximized. A jagged hole was blown in the fuselage, producing the loud whooshing sound of sudden decompression. All the air from inside the plane was rushing outside into the thin atmosphere, and there was none left to sustain life.

In the cockpit, Warner and Rice immediately donned their oxygen masks. So did Holtz and Fagan – but their masks were not supplied. They lost precious time trying vainly to breath before they ripped the masks off and burst into the passenger area, gasping for air. They pulled down masks for themselves and chokingly shouted at their comrades to do the same. In hysteria, Colonel Mao yelled that the wing was on fire. There was a rising shrill of fear and panic as terrorists and hostages alike started finding out that they couldn't breath at all – and the oxygen masks weren't helping.

Warner and Rice hadn't got the jetliner up high enough to carry off Jim Spencer's plan when the shooting incident and the exploding grenade carried it off for them, prematurely. They didn't know exactly what had happened. But they knew they were out in the middle of nowhere. Their left wing was on fire. And they were the only two people on board with air to breath.

They were too far away from the Charlottesville Airport to try and make it there. If they didn't find someplace to land right away, the plane would probably explode. Even if it didn't explode, if it stayed at higher altitudes too long everyone with a useless oxygen mask would either die of anoxia or suffer irreversible brain damage. But the plane couldn't be taken down to breathable levels too rapidly. It had to descend gradually and adjust speed, or else it would go into a nosedive.

As Warner and Rice eased their way closer to the earth, they kept frantically watching the burning wing and looking for a place where they might safely land. All they could see down below were the thickly wooded tops of the Shenandoah Mountains. They needed a large open area, but nothing of the sort was readily apparent. Warner looked at his watch. Too long. Too high. Too much time ticking away before breaking the plane through the clouds.

Then he spotted a broad swath of gas company right-of-way – a road for jeeps and tractors made by bulldozing away trees and brush so that gas lines could be laid right up the side of a steep hill. He lowered the landing gear – it came down with a satisfying clunk, and he was grateful that it hadn't been damaged. As he made his approach, he tried to pick out a relatively level stretch of the right-of-way and hoped it was broad enough not to rip the wings off.

Nosing the plane down, he thought that it was probably too late to save any of the passengers. More than ten minutes had gone by since the explosion.

16

At 6:45 that evening, Vernon and Rose Hearn were still trying to find Carson Manor. 'Their directions aren't worth a damn!' Rose yiped, rapping the backs of her painted nails against the photocopied hand-drawn map supplied by Charles and Anita Walsh. She couldn't understand how she and Vernon had missed the last turn-off that was supposed to put them on the road leading to the Walshes' gravel driveway. For the past hour they had been trying to reorient themselves, retracing their route over a series of narrow, winding, dirt roads with ruts so deep in places that they had to crawl along at less than fifteen miles an hour, their nerves wracked by the bumping and scraping of rocks and hard clay against the underside of their new Cadillac.

Rose took out her compact, flipped it open, and moved the mirror around at various angles to examine her frosted hair. 'Thank God for air-conditioning!' she bleated. 'If I had to sweat and breathe all that road dust and watch my new permanent go all stringy and frizzy, it'd be the last straw!'

'If it weren't for your insistence on a new permanent,' Vernon griped, 'we could've left the house on time and we'd have probably been at Carson Manor three hours ago. As it is, I just hope we get there before dark or we may never find it.'

'Blame it all on me!' Rose snapped. 'You want me to look pretty all the time, yet when I pay some attention to my looks I never hear the end of it!'

'I'm not trying to start an argument, dear,' Vernon said, softening his stand. 'I'm merely making the point that if you had been home packing this morning, instead of running over to the Nautilus Club, you'd have got the message from your hairdresser in time to reschedule an earlier appointment.'

'Now you're on about my exercise classes! I can't believe my ears, Vernon! You ought to be grateful you have a wife who works hard to keep herself attractive for you. Just the other day, my Nautilus instructor guessed my age at twenty-seven.'

'What was he trying to do? Get in your pants?'

'*He's* a woman!'

'Well, I wouldn't be surprised if *she* wanted to get in your pants. Most of those broads who pump iron all the time are a bunch of lezzies. They don't even *look* like women with all those muscles bulging all over the place. Jumping in bed with one of them'd be like jumping in bed with a guy.'

Her hurt feeling dominating her anger, Rose said timidly, 'Are you telling me I look old?'

Vernon hadn't meant to hit her in this sore spot, which was actually a sore spot for them both since they were both obsessed with looking and acting young. In a soothingly sincere tone he said, 'Of course you look young for your age, Rose, I'm not saying you don't. I only meant I wouldn't figure you for twenty-seven. If I didn't know you, I'd probably say about thirty-two or thirty-three.'

'Really?'

'Yeah. You definitely don't look any older than early thirties.'

'Christie Brinkley is twenty-nine,' said Rose. 'So I guess thirty-two isn't so bad.' She had latched on to the figure as though it had suddenly become her true age.

'How old do you think I look?' asked Vernon, setting his jaw and putting on a cheerful expression as he drove, with the idea of enhancing his youthfulness. But a particularly bad bump in the road clanked his teeth together and made him curse. 'Damn! All we have to do is drop the transmission and we'll be stuck out in the middle of these boondocks forever!'

'Thirty-five,' said Rose, lying for the sake of stroking Vernon's ego. She knew that was what he thought he could pass for. He was actually forty-four. Her true opinion was that he looked maybe forty. His stomach was flat and his chest was hard from doing situps and pushups. But his hair was thinning and receding, although it wasn't grey at the sideburns anymore because he was colouring it.

He said, 'A young chick at lunch the other day took me for twenty-nine.'

'Oh?' Rose accused, arching her plucked, pencilled eyebrows. 'What were you doing taking a young chick to lunch?'

'Don't get jealous. She's a production assistant from the new ad agency the boss hired. She's only twenty-three. I'm not bragging, but I think she found me attractive.'

'Well, forget it, she's young enough to be your daughter.'

'So?' Vernon laughed, teasing his wife. 'I can't help it if the young stuff still goes for me.'

'Just as long as you don't go for *it*,' Rose warned jokingly, 'or you might drive me into the arms of my Nautilus instructor.'

They both laughed. Truth was, they were each carrying on extramarital affairs with people younger than themselves. And even though they were vain and jealous of each other in a certain sense, in that each wanted to be the one who looked youngest, neither one deeply cared what the other was doing extramaritally, as long as discretion kept suspicion from hardening into outright confirmation.

'Speaking of young stuff,' Rose said, 'how do you

suppose Sandra and Billy will get along while we're gone?'

Sandra was the Hearns' sixteen-year-old daughter and Billy was her one-year-old son out of wedlock. They were living with Vernon and Rose while Sandra was trying to finish a course at a business school with the hope of becoming a paralegal assistant.

'It's only four days,' said Vernon. 'They should be able to make it on their own for that length of time.'

'I hope she remembers to bathe him,' said Rose. 'It's bad enough he doesn't have a father, he's got a mother who's practically a baby herself! I'm always picking up after her. The other day she skipped Billy's bath because she said she had to study – so *I* ended up bathing the poor child.'

'Well, she has quite a load on her,' Vernon said.

'Don't defend her – she brought it on herself. Couldn't keep her legs together for a few more years.'

'I know, but – '

'But she's driving us both crazy, and you know it. We wouldn't need a psychiatrist if it wasn't for Sandra. It's one thing to come to terms with what she's done and to show her love and support, the way Dr Walsh keeps advising. But what about *us?* Just at a time in our marriage when we should be free to start enjoying ourselves, after sacrificing to raise one kid, we end up with *two* on our hands!'

'It'll only be for a while longer, till she graduates from business school.'

'If she lands a job. And if it pays anything – which it won't. She'll have to keep boarding with us till she traps some guy who doesn't mind a ready-made family.'

Vernon cleared his throat but held his tongue. The subject depressed him and he wanted to let it drop.

Rose began using her compact mirror to inspect her throat, looking for signs of worsening wrinkles. She hadn't mentioned it to her husband yet, but she was seriously considering starting to put aside money for a face-lift, in case she might want one in a few years.

'I recognize where we are now,' said Vernon. 'The road's smoothing out a bit. Right around the next bend, past that tumbled-down barn, is the gas company right-of-way. Remember? It's on the map, right?'

'Yes . . . yes, right here,' said Rose, moving her finger over the map. 'The right-of-way . . . then the stone quarry.'

Both sides of the dirt road were heavily wooded and dense with weeds. The Cadillac came around the tight bend about a hundred yards from the swath of right-of-way that cut through the woods and up the side of a steep hill. He didn't see what was lying in the middle of the road till he was almost on top of it. Just in time he slammed on the brakes and screeched the car to a halt.

'My God! What is it?' Rose shrieked.

'A m-man . . . a b-body,' Vernon stammered.

'Is he . . ?'

'I don't know. We'll have to look. He might need help – first aid or something.'

'We can't just leave the car in the middle of the road.'

'We'll have to. There's no place to pull it over. There hasn't been any traffic anyway.'

Vernon squinted through the windshield, but he couldn't see the body in the road because it was beneath the hood, too close to his front wheels. He hoped he hadn't hit it, but he didn't think so – he hadn't felt that kind of bump.

He opened his door to get out. Just then the 'body' arose, pulling itself up by grabbing on to the bumper and grille. Vernon and Rose stared. It was a shocking sight. A bearded young man in tee shirt and jeans, bleeding profusely from his nose and ears – shoulders and chest splattered with bright red blood. The man's eyes had a dazed, vacant look. He reeled and almost collapsed, but held on to the hood ornament with one hand to keep himself from falling.

'Vernon!' Rose gasped.

Mr Hearn wanted to do something but he didn't know what.

The dazed, bleeding man staggered around the side of the car, holding on with one hand. Then he raised the other hand – and pointed a pistol. Vernon barely had time to realize it was about to go off before it fired at him at point-blank range, blowing half his face away.

Rose started screaming, covering her face with her hands. The assailant poked his arm in, past Vernon's slumped body, and pumped two shots into Rose's face and head, shooting through her fingers and hands. She slammed against the side window, then sank sideways on to the car seat, her newly frosted permanent blown to an oozing pulp.

The assailant stared blankly at what he had done. Then he got into the Cadillac, behind the wheel, shoving Vernon's corpse towards the middle of the front seat. He fumbled with the gearshift till it slipped into 'drive'. Then he stepped on the gas. Hard. The car lurched out, picking up speed. Faster and faster it went, churning dirt and rocks into a screaming cloud of dust. The car was going way too fast to make the bend. But it still kept accelerating.

The Cadillac left the road going sixty or seventy miles per hour, crashing through tall weeds, then mowing down saplings. The man behind the wheel watched all this destruction, his eyes glazed, his foot pressing hard on the accelerator. The car left the ground finally, sailing down into the pit of the old rock quarry – bouncing, crashing, flipping over, and bursting into flames.

The driver – who had been hurled by the impact part

way through the windshield, and then decapitated by jagged glass as the roof crushed in on him – was as dead as his two passengers and did not scream while they were all being incinerated.

17

At seven o'clock that evening Janie Stone was watering the garden as she had done the evening before. She had fed the dog Blackie a tin of pork rinds and a ham hock that her mother had used to make their supper of ham and beans.

Janie was sulking because once again she had been denied a chance – an unexpected one – to go to Carson Manor. Her father had stopped by to wolf down his ham and beans at around four o'clock and had suggested to Sarah that Janie could ride along with him, help him load up the truck with groceries at Carsonville, and help him unload it at the Manor. 'You'll have Brenda and Meredith to lend a hand over there, you don't need Janie,' Sarah had said. 'There still hasn't been nary a drop of rain, and I was figurin' on her waterin' the vegetables again for me.'

Janie liked going to Carsonville about as much as she liked going to the Manor, so it hurt twice as much not to be allowed to go to either place. She was missing out on the bustle of excitement that she always felt in the town and the thrill of looking at all the great stuff in the stores and the shop windows.

Besides, she would have loved not to have to stick around here, in a stone's throw of her grandma. She had been badly shaken when the old lady had clamped her bony fingers around her wrists and had kept yelling about great big snakes coming to kill everybody. '*Hush!* Hush, child!' Sarah had snapped when Janie stumbled downstairs, her face streaked with tears, to tell what Grandma had said and done to her. 'You know,' Sarah had said, 'that she can't get over that blacksnake that fell on her head in the shanty.'

But Janie knew that lots of things Grandma had said had come true. Everybody said so. What if Daddy was going to get killed if he handled a snake in the services come Sunday? Or what if Janie was going to get bit when she worked in the garden? All afternoon she had been fidgety, taking extra care to look where she stepped with her hoe, half expecting a rattler or a copperhead to jump on her. She was sure she'd be watching every move she made for weeks – or *forever* – because how could she ever be satisfied that time had run out on the prediction?

One thing was for sure: she wasn't going to touch any serpents when she went to church – if she lived till then. Maybe she had been toying with the idea before, but Grandma had knocked it out of her head for good. Now she had to convince Daddy to stay away from the snake box. But he probably wouldn't listen. He was too proud and stubborn. He had to prove Mommy was wrong for saying that the devil had a hold of him.

All of a sudden Blackie let out a loud bark, dropping the gristly ham hock he had been chewing and running back towards the woods till his heavy chain jerked him to a dead stop. Janie whirled around. Blackie kept up the most ferocious barking and growling, trying to break his chain in two and fly at whatever he sensed back in the underbrush.

If something was there Janie couldn't hear it – Blackie was making too much racket. Then some foliage parted, and a big greasy-haired behemoth staggered towards her, out of shadows into sunlight. He stopped. She dropped the still-spurting garden hose, ready to bolt and run. Then she saw that the big man was hurt. He looked like a soldier, but he didn't have any rifle. The sleeves of his camouflage shirt were ripped off at the shoulders, exposing huge, hairy, tattooed arms. He was bleeding from his nose and ears. Blood was dripping plop-plop on the grass as he limped towards Janie, babbling, 'Please . . . don't . . . don't run away . . . please . . . help me . . .'

She took a step toward him. Then she saw what one of the tattoos on his arms really was: a coiled green snake with long, needle-sharp fangs. She froze. The man lunged towards her. She backed away. The man came forwards, moving like a zombie. His eyes were glazed. Blood kept plopping on the grass. Janie had now backed up to where Blackie could protect her. But the man didn't seem to notice. When he got within range, Blackie attacked, leaping with a savage throaty growl and clamping his powerful jaws around the big man's upper arm. The man screamed and fell, and the dog hung on, dragging him, trying to rip his arm off.

'Blackie! Blackie!' Janie yelled. There was something about the utter helplessness of the man in the grip of the watchdog that made her lose her fear of him and take pity. She grabbed Blackie's chain and yanked hard, trying to make him let go – but he wouldn't – he dug his paws into the grass and bit down harder than ever. Janie pulled on the chain in a desperate tug-of-war, choking the dog and yelling, 'Blackie! *Blackie! Stop!*' At the same time, the man on the ground swung his free arm in a judo chop across the side of the dog's face and neck. Blackie yipped and let go – and Janie took advantage of the moment by dragging him sideways, away from his quarry.

The man crawled out of reach of the dog. Then he collapsed, bleeding profusely from his left arm now, as well as his ears and nose.

'Blackie! You stay!' Janie yelled. But the dog didn't obey. As soon as Janie dropped the chain, the dog charged till it straightened with a loud clank and kept throwing himself against it – barking, growling, and salivating – in a frenzy to sink his teeth into the wounded man.

By this time, the commotion had brought Sarah Stone out of the house. Wiping her hands on her apron, she stared from the back porch, trying to figure out what was happening.

'Mommy! Help me!' Janie shouted. She ran towards her mother, gasping, 'A man . . . over there . . . hurt!'

Sarah followed Janie out to where the big man lay on his back, apparently unconscious. 'He was already hurt and bleeding when he came out of the woods,' Janie explained. 'And then Blackie jumped on him and bit his arm.'

'My God!' Sarah blurted.

All the while, the watchdog kept yammering and yipping and yanking on his chain, his yellowish eyes fastened on the man's throat, where he longed to sink his fangs.

'We'll have to get this man's wounds cleaned and bandaged,' Sarah said. 'Do you think you and me can move him?'

'Maybe if we drag him,' Janie said. 'I'm scared Blackie's gonna bust loose.'

'He looks awful heavy, but we better try,' said Sarah.

They each grabbed one of the big man's combat boots and started pulling. He was well over six feet tall and weighed close to three hundred pounds. It was all that Janie and Sarah could do to drag him the hundred feet or so from where Blackie was chained up to a shady spot under an elm tree near the back of the house.

'We'll never lift him up the porch steps,' Sarah huffed. 'Better leave him here for now. I'll go in and get the first-aid stuff.'

Sweaty and out of breath, Janie glanced anxiously towards the doghouse, half expecting Blackie to come charging across the yard. He was still barking and growling, but to her relief he seemed to have quieted down some.

She looked down at the wounded man with a mixture

of awe and fear. His left bicep was torn to bloody shreds. His ears and nose were crusted with rivulets of dried blood. The tattoo of a green snake was on his right bicep, but it couldn't be seen right now because of the way that arm had flopped back behind his head when he was being dragged.

Janie had a plausible notion of why the man was dressed up almost like a soldier. She figured he must be a poacher. Men who hunted deer out of season sometimes wore camouflage clothes – forsaking the safety of orange hunting outfits – so as not to be easily spotted by game wardens. To Janie's way of thinking, if this man was doing something wrong like that, God may have punished him by letting him have a bad accident.

The Stones didn't have a regular first-aid kit but just an old shoebox full of things like iodine, gauze, bandages, cotton swabs, and rubbing alcohol. Sarah came out of the house with it and knelt over the fallen man. 'Are you sure he's still breathing?' she asked Janie. 'He looks . . .' She didn't say the word 'dead' out loud. Instead she set down the shoebox full of first-aid stuff and laid her ear against the man's huge, hairy chest to try to hear his pulse.

All of a sudden his eyes popped open – and he seized Sarah by the throat. A mad look on his face, he choked her so hard that her tongue came out and her eyes bulged. Then he rolled her over, still choking, the blood from his nose and ears dripping on to her reddening face.

'Mommy! *Mommy!*' Janie screamed.

The big man kept strangling Sarah, babbling, 'Fascist . . . imperialist . . . fucking . . . pig . . .' as his thick, hairy fingers squeezed harder and harder. His eyes had a mindlessly insane look. Sarah clawed feebly at his wrists, the sudden ferociousness of his assault so overpowering that she was rapidly losing consciousness and the will to resist.

Rooted in her tracks for several critical seconds, Janie now leapt upon the attacker, crying and screaming, pounding and scratching at his back and arms, trying to save her mother. But none of her efforts seemed to have the least effect. The man kept on choking and strangling, as if he and Sarah were the only two people in the yard.

'Blackie! *Blackie! Sic* him, boy!' Janie cried in desperation. But the dog couldn't break his chain and attack though he kept barking and growling and flinging himself forwards till his heavy collar snapped him back.

Janie scratched at the big man's eyes, her nails tearing out deep grooves of bleeding flesh. But he still wouldn't let go of Sarah's throat. 'Fascist . . . fucking . . . *pig!*' he cursed in a spray of bloody spittle. Sarah's arms hung limply, her tongue fat and purple, but he still kept choking. Then he jerked and twisted her like a rag doll.

Janie heard a loud crack and realized with sickening horror that her mother's neck had snapped. She saw the killer releasing Sarah's lifeless form and letting her head smack the ground.

Backing away on rubbery legs, Janie emitted a gut-wrenching moan of agony and despair. The killer turned towards her, his eyes wild, his face raked in crimson streaks. For a long moment, Janie couldn't get her feet moving. The man shuffled towards her in his slow, zombie-like gait. Then she started to run.

Blackie. Blackie would protect her as he had tried to do in the first place.

Huffing and puffing, she tore across the yard as fast as her legs would carry her. Blackie jumped up on her and she unfastened his leash, her trembling fingers fumbling with the catch.

'*Sic* him!' Janie cried in a hoarse, terrified voice.

Slavering and growling, the dog charged the lumbering, three-hundred-pound killer and leapt for his throat. But the man put his arms up, warding off the impact of the dog's plummeting body, and they both fell to the ground. Janie saw that Blackie had managed to chomp down on the killer's right hand. The man let out a mighty roar as he kicked and flailed, but the dog wouldn't let go. '*Get* him, Blackie! *Kill* him!' Janie cried.

But the big oaf was incredibly strong and seemingly almost impervious to pain. Lumberingly powerful, he got up into a kneeling position, simply letting the dog hang on to his hand . . . as if he didn't mind. Blackie dug his paws into the ground and kept tugging and biting for all he was worth. But the man seemed even stronger now, as if his former spell of unconsciousness had infused him with a secret form of energy – a madman's energy. Slowly he pulled the struggling dog towards him, his bitten hand dripping blood. Instinctively, Blackie kept pulling against the man's strength, jerking and twisting his head, trying to get a better grip with his fangs. But then the man punched Blackie full in the face with his free hand and with the bitten one pulled the dog's face down to the ground. At the same time, the man thudded both knees into the dog's side, cracking his ribs.

Janie shrieked, '*Blackie!*' – and started to run.

The whimpering, defeated dog had let go of the man's hand and was feebly trying to crawl away. On his feet now, the man stomped his combat boot down hard across Blackie's neck, splintering the bones, and with a final yelp the animal died.

The big killer turned around slowly, looking to where Janie was headed. He saw her running past her mother's dead body and up the steps of the back porch.

Janie could hear the slow, plodding footsteps and the loud, raspy breathing of the monstrous man who was pursuing her as she slammed the back door shut and fumbled with the bolt. The living room door – for all she knew, it might be unlocked. She started towards it, then changed her mind, yanked open a sink drawer, and pulled out a long, sharp butcher's knife. At that same instant the back door crashed in on her in a shower of splinters, and the demented killer glowered at her as he came striding through. He didn't seem to see the knife that she held in her hand or else he didn't care at all about it. He lunged at her and seized her by the throat, as he had done to her mother. Choking her, he lifted her off the floor as if he wished to gaze into her eyes as they attained the glaze of death – the same glaze that his own eyes already possessed. With all her remaining strength, she swung the butcher's knife in an upwards arc and heard his breath whoosh as the blade punctured the soft flesh of his fat upper belly. With a sick roar, he dropped her and she scrambled to her feet. Astounded, she saw him pull the long knife out of his stomach and drop it as if he had removed a splinter.

He shambled relentlessly after her as she hurtled through the living room and out the front door.

On the porch, the big killer turned slowly this way and that, looking for where Janie might be headed. He gave an oafishly smug grunt of satisfaction when he spied her running into an old, sagging, weatherbeaten barn. Then he staggered down the porch steps, his abdomen leaking blood and visceral fluid while his other wounds also continued to bleed.

Janie saw her attacker coming closer as she struggled to pull the heavy barn door shut. It was hanging askew on its rusty hinges, one corner dug into the ground, embedded in tall weeds. Janie pulled with all her might but it wouldn't budge. Over her shoulder she glimpsed the killer's broad, greasy, blood-streaked face contorted in rage. She didn't think she could survive if she had to keep running from him. He was only ten or fifteen feet away when she kicked and kicked at a tuft of dirt and weeds and sprung the door loose from its mooring. With her assailant almost in reach of her, the swinging door obliterated his fat, ugly face just in time. Even as it did so, she saw that the hinges were so rusty and weak that the bolts were pulling away from the rotting wood. But it was too late now, she'd have to hope that the door would hold. She found the heavy wooden bar and slammed it down into the L-shaped brackets. She flipped the switch, and in the dull, dusty illumination provided by one naked overhead bulb she ran past rotting bales of straw and a tangle of rusty barnyard junk to the side door, and made sure it was locked.

Her heart was pounding and she was gasping so hard she thought her chest would burst as she crept through the dusty, junk-filled barn looking for a hiding place. She knew that the search was bound to be futile; there was no way she could remain permanently hidden once the killer came in after her. And he was roaring and hammering on the big door so hard that the bolts on the rusty hinges were already starting to rip through the rotten jamb.

Her eyes fell on the one naked lightbulb. It was hanging above the steps to the loft. She picked up an old piece of two-by-four. Then she scampered up the steps, and when she got to the top she used the two-by-four to smash out the light.

She cowered in the loft. She thought of her dead mother, and of her grandmother alone in the house, and of the tattooed serpent on the killer's arm. In a way, Grandma had been right: *Great big snakes a-comin' to kill us*.

The roaring and pounding kept up incessantly. Peeking down from the loft, Janie saw a crack of light widening as one of the hinges tore completely loose. She ducked back, wishing she could just burrow in the straw and melt away to nothing so she couldn't be found and killed. But it was like trying to escape one of the monsters in her nightmares – nothing seemed to work, except waking up.

But this was nothing she could wake up from. It was too horrifyingly real.

All she had was a two-by-four to defend herself with. If the big man started to climb the steps to the loft, she'd have to try conking him on the head – but she didn't really believe she could stop him that way when he had somehow been able to ignore a butcher's knife in his gut. There was another great ripping sound, a grunt, and a crash. Light came flooding into the barn, some of it spilling up towards the loft. Janie dropped her two-by-four. She saw something better gleaming in the straw. Her fingers closed around it as the killer's hoarse, rasping breath and heavy, plodding footsteps came closer . . . and closer.

The big man mumbled: 'Fascist . . . pig . . . fascist . . . pig . . .'

When he stopped mumbling and stopped stumbling around, the only sound was the plop-plopping of his blood dripping from his wounds. As if the sound enraged him, he let out a raspy roar and started heaving pieces of junk out of his way. When his tantrum ceased, his breathing was hoarser and raspier than ever. Then he gave a little snort – like the self-satisfied snort of a predator who has at last found his prey. He mumbled, 'Fascist pig . . . fascist . . . pig . . .' Then he started climbing the steps to the loft. Slowly . . . slowly . . . he hoisted his enormous bulk till at last his glassy, insane-looking eyes peered over the threshold.

Suddenly – a flash of a pitchfork – and the fat gleaming tines buried themselves in the killer's throat. Screaming, he fell to the floor of the barn, his hands choking the handle of the pitchfork, trying to pull it out. His blood was pumping from his jugular in bright, three-foot-high spurts as Janie scrambled down out of the loft and ran past him. The spurts got smaller and smaller as she looked back over her shoulder at the dying monster.

113

On her way towards the house she cried hysterically, 'Grandma . . . Grandma!'

Just then, a staccato burst of machine gun fire chipped divots of wood out of the farmhouse. Janie stopped in her tracks and some of the bullets chewed up the dirt around her. She pivoted and ran in the opposite direction. She heard windows shattering – then there was a vicious explosion – and the blast sent Janie pitching on to her face amid flying debris.

Grenades! She had seen enough television that she guessed it must've been grenades. But *why?* Why was all this happening? Lying flat on the ground, Janie risked a look at the house. She was sure that her grandmother couldn't have survived the explosion. But then she saw Grandma, who hadn't walked for six years, emerging through acrid smoke and rubble – one arm a bloody stump. 'Snakes! Snakes!' Mary Monohan shrieked, standing in the doorway like a saint in a flannel nightgown, pointing a long, bony, accusing finger.

Now Janie saw that Grandma was staring straight at three soldiers with green snake armbands – the ones who had destroyed the house. They had mindless, vacant eyes like the monster who had killed Mommy. 'Snakes!' Grandma yelled, and took a step towards them – only to fall into a hole in what was left of the front porch. She struggled to climb out of the ruins. She kept mumbling about snakes, and blood kept spurting from the stump of her arm, till she finally sank down into the dusty hole and did not emerge again.

Janie let out an agonized scream. The three men with guns looked at her with dumb, brutelike curiosity, and they seemed to move in slow motion getting their guns aimed. She took off running again, sure she wouldn't make it this time – but the bullets whined and whistled behind her as if the brutes were too slow and dumb to keep a bead on a moving target. Not believing her luck, she dashed into the woods – then tripped and fell, half stumbling and half crawling to shelter behind a fat stump.

The men kept firing their guns at Janie long after she had effectively hidden herself. She cowered, expecting to die, but the bullets kept crashing and ricocheting all around her. The men continued squeezing the triggers of their weapons even after all the magazines were empty and the firing pins were striking empty chambers . . . click, click . . . click . . . click . . .

18

Jim Spencer knew that the Boeing 747 was down. He had been watching the radar screen as the aeroplane was being tracked from the control tower of the Charlottesville Airport. At 6:15 P.M., when it was roughly a hundred miles away, the plane had begun climbing to high altitude – on schedule. Spencer had felt a rush of excitement, believing that Larry Warner and Dave Rice were going to be able to carry out his plan. But then something had gone wrong. The plane had started sinking and flying an erratic course. Then its radar blip had disappeared from the screen. It had gone down somewhere over the Shenandoah Mountains to the northwest. But Spencer didn't know exactly where or why. The logical explanation would be that Warner and Rice must've aroused the suspicions of the Green Brigade when they took the plane up. Maybe one of the terrorists, finding that he had no oxygen supply, had panicked and started shooting. For whatever reason, the plane was down. Spencer had to try to find it. If it had crashed, there probably wouldn't be any survivors. But there was the barest possibility that it had force landed – and if so, armed terrorists might be loose in the countryside. Even if nothing was left of the flight but strewn wreckage and mutilated corpses, Spencer had to get to the scene ahead of any civilian authorities in order to prevent them from finding out anything about the scheme that had backfired.

It was now 7:28 P.M. Jim Spencer and Sam Bernardi, the FBI agent who had piloted the LearJet that had brought Spencer and his SWAT commandos to Charlottesville, were in an office they had taken over in the airport control tower. The sparsely furnished office had a blue haze of smoke despite the air conditioning. Behind one of the steel desks, Spencer was drinking his fifth cup of coffee from a machine down the hall and was puffing his twelfth cigarette of the hour. Behind the other steel desk, Sam Bernardi – a sour-looking, big-nosed, dark-complected man with deepset black eyes and a black, wiry crewcut – was sipping his fourth carton of lemon blend. He did not smoke at all and did not take coffee or other stimulants when he was on a piloting mission. Depending on how things worked out, he might still have to fly the LearJet, although at the moment it seemed doubtful.

The LearJet was practically useless for reconnaissance over heavily wooded mountainous terrain. Since it couldn't dip and hover, the only way wreckage might be spotted from such an aircraft under such difficult topographical conditions was if the approximate location of the wreckage were known. But radar data wasn't sufficient to pinpoint precisely where the plane might have gone after the blip had vanished, and whatever was left of the 747 could be obscured by dense foliage. Even if something could be spotted from the LearJet, there was hardly any chance of finding enough open, level space for it to land safely. A type of aircraft was needed that could deploy men to investigate the situation or carry out a mop-up operation if any of the terrorists were still alive. That was why Sam Bernardi had suggested the use of helicopters and had requested that four of them be dispatched from the FBI hangar at Dulles Airport in Washington. The SWAT commandos could be broken down into four search teams aboard four choppers. Then they could scour the mountain forests for signs of where Warner and Rice might have gone down.

'If they'd crashed on a farm or near where anybody lives, we'd have received a report by now from civilian authorities,' Spencer said. 'And if Warner and Rice were alive, they would have made it to a phone.'

'Not necessarily,' said Bernardi. 'One of the guys in the control tower told me that some of the really dirt-poor miners and farmers in those mountains don't even have electricity, let alone telephones.'

'What if Warner and Rice got caught trying to pull our little trick?' said Spencer. 'Kintay could've forced them to land in a field somewhere, then had them shot.'

'I don't believe Kintay would cut off his nose to spite his face,' said Bernardi. 'No matter what happened, he'd want to keep that plane in the air. He was bound and determined to get to Cuba so he could hug and kiss his idol, Fidel.'

'You talk as if Kintay is *rational!*' Spencer snapped. 'I wouldn't put *anything* past the bastard. Furthermore, it's conceivable that he could've lost control of his followers. Then Mao or Chu would probably have taken over, and if anything they're crazier than he is.'

'A gang of assholes with grenades and machine guns could wreak terrible havoc on isolated families out in those boondocks,' Bernardi mused.

'Yeah,' said Spencer, leaning back, exhaling a cloud of cigarette smoke. 'Thank God the odds are against that kind of scenario. My hunch is that everybody aboard that plane is dead.'

'That's probably what we'll find,' Bernardi agreed.

Spencer couldn't help thinking that as much as he hated to lose Warner and Rice and twelve more hostages, it would almost be worth it if all the terrorists had also perished in the wreckage of the 747. But it was a far cry from the elegant solution he had envisioned. He had dared to hope that the oxygen deprivation would put the Green Brigade asleep like babies; then the 747 would glide peacefully into Charlottesville to deliver his enemies into his hands. What a story it would have made! Spencer would have been a hero. Not that he cared for that kind of adulation, except for the off-chance it might elicit a smidgeon of respect from his daughter Caroline. But such was not to be. Depending upon what the true situation was out on those mountains, he might end up the goat instead of the hero. His plan may have screwed up badly enough to bring disgrace down upon himself as well as the Bureau. 'When the hell are those choppers gonna get here?' he blurted in his exhaustion and frustration.

'Any minute,' Sam Bernardi said calmly. 'I expect they'll land any minute. I was told they were airborne at 6:45, and Dulles is less than an hour's flight away.'

Bernardi was a practiced stoic who didn't let the unfavourable conclusions he had drawn about Spencer show in his voice. He had flown helicopters on search and destroy missions in Vietnam, where he had learned to evaluate field commanders. Most were highly professional, intelligent men, sensitive to their many responsibilities, including the selection of targets that deserved to be destroyed and could be destroyed without unacceptable risk to their own men or to noncombatants. Some were reckless or stupid. And a few were so coldly ambitious or so overly zealous that their decisions always seemed to lean the way that would produce the highest body count.

In Bernardi's opinion, Jim Spencer was that type of commander. Bernardi didn't trust Spencer's ability to make wise or ethical decisions. The man was strung out on caffeine, nicotine, and lack of sleep. The lack of sleep couldn't be helped, but the other two factors could have been. A man who tortured his nervous system with such massive doses of coffee and cigarettes must have nerves full of demons that he was trying to subdue. Demons that could never be exorcised. Even if Spencer gave them the kind of body count that would make the 'best' out of a bad situation.

In many ways, this mission against the Green Brigade reminded Sam Bernardi of his Vietnam assignments. He was still working against commies, but this time they were on American soil. Whether he happened to be flying a chopper or a LearJet, his job was to get his own troops in and out safely and not to worry about what they did in the interval. He was largely an observer, not a participant. He wasn't going to shoot anybody. He was only going to work the controls of an airborne machine. He had no moral responsibility for whatever happened on the ground. At least that's what he had told himself in Nam on the several occasions when he had seen women and children ripped apart by bullets or sizzled by flamethrowers.

'Listen to me, Sam,' Spencer said, jolting Bernardi out of his reverie. 'I don't want anything about our oxygen-deprivation plan to leak to the news media. They'll start demanding an investigation. All our asses will be in a sling. The damn bleeding hearts will try to crucify us for toying with the hostages' lives. They'll whine that what we did was immoral, unethical, and unnecessary, and that we should have sat tight and let the hostages be released in Havana.'

'Maybe we should have,' Bernardi ventured.

'No way,' said Spencer, lighting another cigarette. His eyes were cold slits, and his voice was stern and adamant. 'No way,' he repeated. 'I wasn't going to let Kintay and his band of communist fanatics get away clean with a two-million-dollar haul. They'd be down in Cuba training more assholes just like themselves to plague us for years to come.'

19

At half past seven, George Stone finished putting away the supplies he had brought from Carsonville. Brenda Meachum, who had been checking stuff off the list and telling him where to put certain items, coaxed him into accepting a plate of leftovers to eat in the kitchen.

'I thought you mentioned that a couple of folks didn't show up yet,' said George. 'I won't be taking food out of their mouths, will I?'

'Oh, bosh! There's plenty for them!' said Brenda. 'Last you ate was almost four hours ago, wasn't it? After you did all that work for us, I'm not going to let you go home with your stomach growling.'

Some of the food looked strange to George, particularly the hot hash and the Indian pudding, and he eyed the side dishes with trepidation as he sat at the big kitchen table. But when he got up the nerve to taste them, he broke into a smile, showing his crooked teeth. 'These vittles is a sight fancier than what a plain man is used to,' he told Brenda. 'I sure hope they stick on my ribs as easy as they go down.'

Brenda knew he was teasing, but she pretended to be insulted, glowering at him with both hands on her fat hips. 'You ain't likely to get better grub than what I cook, George, and you know it. I don't like to brag, but the folks gave me and Meredith an ovation just a while ago.'

The Walshes and their guests were still in the parlour having after-dinner drinks. They were all on their second round of sherry, except for Sanford and Joan Berman, who were sticking with coffee.

Andrea Warnak, Mark and Heather Pearson, and Charles and Anita Walsh were engaged in a rather lively conversation, while everyone else was mostly just listening. The talk was about the Old South and the plantation system. The formal colonial parlour was an appropriate setting for such a topic, and of course Charles Walsh was delighted to expound on matters close to his heart. 'Land was the highest form of property ownership,' he was explaining to everybody. 'The more land a man owned, the higher his social status. Every man aspired to become a planter, and the planters presided over society much in the fashion of the country gentry back home in England.'

'Why did people give them that kind of respect?' Andrea Warnak asked.

'Because,' said Charles, 'in many ways they deserved it. They were proven leaders, proven accomplishers. They had to not only know all about soil and crops and methods of curing, but also be able to mend farming tools, understand meteorology, appraise the value of goods, plus ship and market them wisely, doing a good enough job of investing and bookkeeping so that they didn't drive themselves into bankruptcy.'

'I can see why, with that kind of background, the best of them would be remarkable, extraordinary men,' said Mark Pearson. 'Like Thomas Jefferson.'

'That's for sure,' Charles agreed, smiling and sipping his sherry.

Anita liked to see Charles having a good time. She knew that this was his idea of getting the marriage encounter off to a good start, with a fine meal and some relaxed socializing. He always maintained that one of the best ways of helping couples to heal their differences was to show them they could still have fun in each other's presence.

It was nice to see Mark Pearson unwinding a bit. Apparently he and Charles were starting to hit it off, and Heather was visibly relieved by this development, smiling animatedly at some of the points that were being made.

The only one who didn't appear to be enjoying the discussion, or at least coexisting amicably with it even if it didn't interest him, was Harvey Warnak. As a matter of fact, while Charles was answering one of Andrea's rather bubbleheaded questions about olden times at Carson Manor, Harvey broke in rudely and asked if it would be okay if he went for a walk. He pointedly didn't mean for anyone to join him, especially not Andrea. He spoke politely, but one could tell that underneath he was seething. 'I mean, if we're not going to get down to any serious marriage-encounter business, I'd like to go out for a stroll to work off some of the calories.'

'Certainly,' said Charles.

'Mind if we go with you?' Ben Harris asked. His wife nudged him, and he gave her an annoyed, puzzled look, having missed the signal that Harvey wanted to be alone.

'Actually, I'd rather be by myself,' Harvey said. 'I was thinking that I might add a few lines to the letter we all started this afternoon.'

'Fine, you go right ahead,' said Sophie Harris. 'Maybe Ben and I will just sit on the veranda. We don't get to enjoy much of the outdoors back in Richmond, since we live in one of those retirement high-rises.'

So Harvey went out of the door, and in a little while the Harrises finished their sherry and followed him.

Anita Walsh looked at her watch and wondered for the umpteenth time what could be delaying Vernon and Rose Hearn. They had only been a hundred miles away when they had phoned from the gas station. It didn't seem logical that they would turn around and go home at that point, even if they had had an argument. Maybe their car had broken down. But if so, why wouldn't they place another phone call?

Anita hoped the Hearns hadn't had some sort of dreadful accident. But she didn't mention her fear. No use alarming the other guests. Vernon and Rose would probably turn up by and by. Actually, Anita thought, trying to look on the light side, she wouldn't put it past them to stop off at a disco to prove how 'young at heart' they could still be.

Joan Berman was thinking that she'd like to have a glass of sherry instead of coffee, but abstaining from alcohol was her way of encouraging Sanford to do so. She wished he would show her as much consideration by not eating everything he pleased when she was on a diet. Once again she had over-indulged, but the meal had been resplendent, and if there was one thing she could not stay away from it was good food. Sanford never helped her reduce, but always made fun of her, saying, 'If I'm an alcoholic, you're a foodaholic, and that's almost as bad.' She did not agree. She vividly remembered the hell it had been before he had got his own addiction under control, and she dreaded the hell it would be if he ever fell off the wagon.

She had known about his drinking problem before she married him, but she had naïvely thought she could change him. For thirteen years she had tried, and nothing had worked. Even having four kids had failed to settle him down. In the end, it had taken a bizarre and humiliating incident to bring him to his senses. Joan shuddered inwardly every time she thought of it. All of the ugly details were indelibly engraved in her brain . . .

She and Sanford were at an insurance company convention in Nashville, where he was being honoured as top agent. She had long understood that one of the reasons her husband drank was to escape the pressures he put on himself – the burning inner hunger, not only for worldly success but for self-approval, that drove him always to be number one in writing new policies. So she could not be sanguine about his work, and she viewed the awards he earned with mixed feelings – as if they were symbols of what was wrong in their lives, instead of what was right. And she knew he resented her for not being behind him all the way.

Over dinner on the first night of the convention, he imbibed so much vodka that he began to hallucinate. He swore that some of the waiters were carrying guns and knives, flashing them behind the customers' backs. His first remark to this effect sounded like a joke, and everyone laughed nervously, but he didn't drop it. He began to imagine that if he wasn't going to be shot or stabbed, he was going to be poisoned – and halfway through the meal, he got up, smashing glasses and plates on to the floor, and staggered out into the street.

With much desperate pleading and cajoling, Joan managed to get Sanford into bed at their motel, but he awoke five minutes later, screaming that someone had been strangled 'in this very bed' and if he and Joan didn't run for it the murderer would come and strangle them, too. Joan tried to calm him down again, but the wild look in his eyes wouldn't abate, and he kept sipping straight vodka from a bottle he had hidden in his suitcase. At the peak of his drunkenness he insisted on phoning the police, and Joan let him – she figured it was one way of getting help, because she couldn't deal with him any longer. Two uniformed cops arrived to find that they had a babbling lunatic on their hands, stinking of booze and running around in his undershorts. Sanford kept ranting and raving about 'the strangler' and accusing the cops of being part of the 'murder plot' – and they had no choice but to book him for disturbing the peace and being drunk and disorderly.

Today, Joan still didn't know exactly what had gone through Sanford's head or what had been done to him while he was locked up like a crazed animal. He wouldn't talk about it, except to say that it had been the worst night of his life. The horrible night in a jail cell, wrestling with demons of his own making, had apparently transformed him in a way that Joan had never been able to. After that, he was finally ready to admit he was an alcoholic, and with very little additional encouragement from her, he had sought help for his problem. Somehow he had managed to hang on to his job with the insurance company, and he was still a successful agent, though not as successful as before since he wasn't driving himself so hard. He no longer had the compulsion to be number one. And Joan figured it was all the better. She liked the way her life was now, except for its precariousness. She was doing her best to preserve the delicate balance by keeping Sanford in AA and going to counselling with him so Dr Anita Walsh could help him dissect his psyche and get at the roots of his alcoholism.

Cliques, Sanford Berman was thinking. Everywhere you went there had to be cliques, even at a goddamn marriage encounter. The highbrow clique was the Pearsons, the Walshes, and the Warnak broad. The lowbrows were the Bermans, the Harrises, and maybe Harvey Warnak – it was hard to tell because he was so down in the mouth.

Sanford Berman viewed the world basically as two cliques: highbrows and lowbrows. Highbrows were people who were obsessed with being correct and proper – they acted like they never had to go to the toilet. Lowbrows were unpolished, they had rough edges – they were real people.

In the insurance business, the highbrows dealt mainly

with corporations; the lowbrow agents, like Sanford Berman, sold to the average guy.

All his life, Sanford had never been accepted by the highbrows, even when he showed them up by registering a consistently bigger sales volume. No matter how many awards he won, they still looked down on him. They were the highbrows, he was the lowbrow. They could be impressed with themselves for landing a few fat commissions on wealthy, prestigious accounts, while he outgrossed them by piling up hundreds of small ones. He used to need courage out of a bottle, not to stop himself from feeling inferior, but to blunt his awareness that they thought he was.

Today he had made his same old mistake of trying to ingratiate himself with the highbrows. The Walshes had chuckled under their breath when he had tried to tell them how to turn a good buck off of their hoity-toity old-time plantation. The Warnak broad had called him crass and ignorant.

He had half a notion to get hammered, for the first time in over a year, and tell all the highbrows to go to hell.

But when the itch to have a drink came on him, he always thought about what had really happened in that jail cell in Nashville. He had put it all in his letter to his wife, but damned if he would ever let her read it. He had never told anybody the awful truth, not even the people at Alcoholics Anonymous. He wasn't about to tell his wife or the Walshes.

The shrinks were like Peeping Toms waiting for a man to bare his soul. They loved looking at pus. To get to see it, they pushed the idea that a man had to lance his wounds and purge them right in front of everybody. But Sanford Berman wasn't buying their spiel. He was two steps ahead of them. He was doing all right. For over a year he had stayed sober, while carrying his secret on his own shoulders.

The worst thing that had happened in the jail cell wasn't the d.t.s. It wasn't the first time Sanford had wrestled with the green rats and pink snakes of his subconscious, even though this time they had taken a different form, that of a human killer coming after him. Through counselling, he pretty much understood now that his booze nightmares were manifestations of his intense fear of failure – a phobia that drove him to attack the world as if everything in it were trying to strangle him. He detested the idea of being thought of as a failure.

And that's how he thought of himself when he slept off the d.t.s. and awoke in his own vomit in a cage fit for a rat. It was like the highbrows were finally proved right: he didn't deserve their respect or anybody else's. He was the lowest, meanest, filthiest, and dumbest creature on the face of the earth. After this escapade, everybody – even his wife and children – would hold him in utter and well-earned contempt.

Faced with his disgrace and his complete loss of self-esteem, he realized that he didn't want to go on living. His wife and kids would be better off without him; he wasn't worth the face value of his whole-life policy. He fashioned a noose out of his vomit-stained shirt and tied it around the bars of his cell. With strips of tee shirt he tied his wrists and ankles together so he couldn't try to save himself. He put his head in the noose and jumped from his steel cot, thinking that he might break his neck or at least knock himself out – then he started to suffocate. Suddenly it wasn't what he wanted to do. He tried to scream for help, but only a few weak, strangled sounds would come out. He kicked and flailed at the bars, but he was so trussed up he couldn't make much noise, and every time he jerked and twisted the noose got tighter. Finally, he blacked out.

He came to on the cold concrete floor of the cell, in his own vomit puddle once again. His neck hurt. So did other parts of his body from banging against the bars.

The cell warden checking the prisoners on his hourly rounds had found Sanford Berman near death and had cut him down. To Sanford's horror, the man said he would have to report the suicide attempt. But he ended up taking a bribe of a thousand dollars not to do so. 'It's your funeral, hoss,' the cell warden had drawled. 'I guess I don't mind if you bump yourself off after you leave here, as long as you don't do it in my jail, on my shift.'

Sanford had discovered how little he really thought of himself and how badly he wanted to live even though he might not deserve to. He wanted to try to do better. He wanted to see his kids grow up, get married, and give him grandchildren.

He was terrified that his wife and kids might leave him if they ever found out how much of a coward he had been. That's why he constantly bullied Joan and made fun of her for being fat, while at the same time he really didn't want to see her lose weight. He wanted her to stay addicted to food, the way he was addicted to alcohol. He wanted her to carry the evidence of her addiction around with her in the form of excess poundage, so she wouldn't get to feeling that she was better than he was and didn't need him anymore.

He understood why he mistreated Joan – intellectually he understood it – but emotionally he couldn't stop himself. He didn't think that telling her or anybody else about his suicide attempt would help. It was enough that *he* knew about it. It was serving its purpose, wasn't it? The scary memory of it was what had kept him on the wagon for over a year.

In a lachrymose mood, Harvey Warnak walked around the side of the house towards the stable. He didn't want to hang around the front yard since the Harrises had said they were going to sit on the veranda. He didn't want anyone to intrude on his thoughts. He just wanted to be alone so he could sulk and feel sorry for himself without being nagged for it and without anybody making any kind of misguided attempt to cheer him up.

He walked past the beautiful palominos in the corral without giving them more than a glance. He kept going, to behind the stable where the excavated outlines of the old slave cabins could be seen in the ground. He kicked at some of the embedded brick fragments, even though his conscience told him he shouldn't do it, he should have more respect for his hosts' efforts at archeology. But it wasn't something he truly gave a damn about, even though he often pretended to be interested, for Andrea's sake. He cared about the things that made today's world tick, for instance the computer programs and designs that he helped build, rather than the images of a vanished past that his wife loved to study and dream about.

Tormented by a belated, profound sensitivity to the many differences between himself and Andrea, he was nevertheless morose over his inability to fall as deeply in love with her as he had once been, and he was jealous over her obvious romantic attraction to Charles Walsh. The irony was that he didn't want to lose her while there was still hope that their relationship could be rebuilt, yet his belief in that happy outcome was at a terribly low ebb.

He wondered if maybe her near-fatal illness and his supposed rejection of her at that time was really, fundamentally, beside the point. Perhaps their marriage had been a mistake in the first place, destined to end in divorce even if the ordeal with the brain operation had never occurred. Maybe the tumour was a cruel trick of fate, designed to make Harvey feel even more guilty for falling out of love with Andrea.

Maybe the true problem was that Harvey and Andrea didn't have enough in common. Much as it hurt him to admit it, he believed more and more that his wife could have been happier married to someone like Charles Walsh. Someone who shared her fascination with art and literature.

In the beginning, it had been fun to explain themselves as a couple by joking that opposites attract. Maybe that was true for a short fling, but it didn't hold water over the long haul. Common ground was the important thing. Without enough of it, opposites would eventually repel.

Harvey patted the letter to his wife that was in his suit jacket. In it he had written most of the rambling thoughts and torments that were now playing through his mind like a mournful reprise. Kicking at a clump of dirt, he started to walk along a wooded path leading away from the site of the slave cabins. He was making up his mind to show his letter to Andrea. Maybe he would do it tonight, after they retired to their room.

As he walked past a large tree, his mind absorbed in his problems, an arm reached out for him and a hand clamped over his mouth. Wide-eyed, he saw the flash of the sharp bayonet in the instant before it was drawn across his throat, severing the jugular vein, causing blood to erupt in bright, pulsating spurts.

Mickey Holtz and Janet Fagan – the two Green Brigade terrorists who had been in the cockpit of the Boeing 747 with the pilot and copilot – knelt down beside Harvey Warnak and stabbed him over and over. With looks of brutish glee in their eyes, they methodically and mind-lessly continued their stabbing long after Harvey was dead.

'The society of the Old South,' said Charles Walsh, 'was based on the harshest kind of inequality – human slavery. But the irony was that the planter class, the aristocracy, had a deep sense of public service and a devotion to the ideals of democracy. Washington and Jefferson were both slaveholders, yet Jefferson wrote that all men are created equal, and Washington fought and won the war based on that principle.'

'Well, only one in four families held slaves,' said Andrea.

'That's not the point,' said Mark Pearson. 'What Charles is saying is – '

He was interrupted by a piercing scream from the veranda.

A perplexed look on his face, Charles got up and went to the door. Sophie Harris screamed again. When Charles opened the door he saw Ben and Sophie cowering behind a white pillar before he realized what they were cowering from.

The .45 automatic that had been pointed at them was now pointed at him.

General Kintay, the Green Brigade leader that Charles had seen on TV, was standing at the foot of the veranda steps. 'My God!' Charles gasped as he was hit with the shock of recognition mixed with a jumble of images from his nightmare and the vivid recall of Mary Monohan's prediction.

Kintay was bleeding from the nose and had an evil, vacant look in his eyes. He seemed to need all his concentration to hold the .45 steady at the end of a limply extended arm. Before he could pull the trigger, he collapsed, hitting the courtyard bricks with a dull thud.

By that time, the rest of the people had followed Charles out to the veranda. As he started down the steps towards Kintay, Anita yelled, 'Charles! Stay back!'

But Charles took away the .45 that was loosely clutched in Kintay's fingers. Then he peeled back the terrorist leader's eyelids and looked into his empty-seeming eyes. 'He's out cold. I'll watch him closely, Anita, I've got his gun. You go and get George Stone to help me carry this man into the house.'

'But he was going to *shoot* us!' wailed Sophie Harris from behind a pillar.

'What is he?' asked Joan Berman. 'A-a soldier?'

'A terrorist,' Charles said succinctly. 'He calls himself General Kintay.'

'Well I'll be!' Sanford Berman bellowed. 'I saw a thing about him on the news last night. Leader of the so-called Green Brigade. They robbed a bank in New York and were demanding a plane to take them to Cuba.'

'Right,' said Charles. 'I saw the broadcast too. Their plane must've come down somewhere near here, for some reason. Anita, go and get George. Let's take Kintay into the house. We've got to do what we can for him medically, then turn him over to the police.'

'I'll give you a hand,' said Mark Pearson.

'He's going to be heavy,' said Charles. 'He's dead weight. Better wait for George to pitch in.'

Andrea Warnak had a stricken look on her face. 'Harvey . . . he's out there somewhere,' she said in a fearful whisper.

Charles sniffed the barrel of Kintay's .45. 'Chances are Harvey's okay,' he said with more conviction than he felt. 'This gun hasn't been fired.'

'I didn't hear any shots,' said Sanford Berman.

'But . . . from what you say, there may be other terrorists out there,' said Andrea.

When George Stone came from the kitchen, he and Charles supported Kintay's upper body, and Mark Pearson and Sanford Berman grabbed hold of his legs. 'Be careful, Mark,' Heather Pearson said before following Anita Walsh, Andrea Warnak, Joan Berman, and Sophie Harris into the parlour. Ben Harris held the door open as the other four men carried Kintay bodily up the veranda steps.

Just then, Colonel Mao limped around the side of the house and saw her lover being 'captured'. She immediately opened fire with an automatic rifle, apparently without considering that she might easily kill the man she was trying to 'save'. But her use of the weapon was so slow and clumsy that she hit nobody. A few bullets ricocheted off the marble pillars while the men ran into the house, dragging Kintay with them.

Two more terrorists stepped up beside Colonel Mao and, taking their cue from her, they opened fire. Bullets shattered windows and blasted out chunks of bricks, mortar and marble.

'Hit the floor! Stay low, everybody!' Charles Walsh yelled, slamming the door and bolting it even while bullets were flying. He whirled and tackled Joan Berman, who had frozen, pushing her down behind the arm of a sofa. Everyone else was ducking and hiding. Mark Pearson had fallen on top of Heather, protecting her with his body. Anita reached out and touched Charles's fingers to let him know she hadn't been hit; he had felt a surge of dread when he first saw her lying flat in a corner. 'Meredith! Brenda!' Charles bellowed. 'Lock everything up!' Keeping as low as possible, he started crawling out of the parlour to help secure other areas.

Cringing on the floor, Sanford Berman saw Charles manoeuvre past him, zigzagging sideways like a soldier going under barbed wire. Sanford wondered how Charles could do this when he himself didn't have the nerve to move. He didn't think he could get up even if he knew for sure that one of the bullets was going to find him right where he lay. Then, as Charles's legs wriggled through the doorway, Sanford was able to see something in the corner that had been obstructed from his view: the liquor cabinet. He needed what was inside. But he didn't dare reach out for it. It kept calling to him. But he felt that if he moved he'd get shot. And if a bullet didn't destroy him, the alcohol would.

The racket of gunfire kept up, splintering glass and chipping out puffs of plaster. Precious antiques were being ripped to pieces.

Joan Berman and Sophie Harris were both crying.

Sanford Berman reached for the door of the liquor cabinet . . . then forced himself to pull his arm back.

Kintay came to and started shrieking and babbling half coherent nonsense about 'the beast of fascism' and 'the pig holocaust'. Mark Pearson and George Stone pushed him down and held him, then used his bootlaces to bind his wrists and ankles. At the top of his lungs he shrieked, 'Fascist pigs! Fascist *pigs! Burn* in the *flames* of freedom!' His delirious outburst seemed to spark the fusillade to a greater frenzy.

It was the final straw for Sanford Berman, his willpower was broken. He opened the liquor cabinet and seized a bottle of bourbon, hugging it close to his face, staring at the amber liquid and the artfully scrawled label. He told himself he shouldn't do this, he played through his mind some of the sayings and preachings from Alcoholics Anonymous. But it was one thing to hear those things at a meeting and another to believe in them under fire. He screwed the cap off the bourbon and started swigging.

Kintay kept screaming and thrashing. 'Fascist *pigs! Burn* in the flames of freedom!'

'Let's gag him!' Mark Pearson shouted.

George Stone yanked a red bandana from his coverall pocket and crammed it in the terrorist leader's mouth.

Sanford Berman gulped more bourbon.

Crawling through the dining room, Charles Walsh found that the gunfire was even heavier on that side of the house. Paintings were being riddled. Plates and ornaments of fine china and porcelain were being powdered to dust. As Charles crawled through broken shards, a staccato eruption sent the crystal chandelier crashing on to what was left of the long, gracefully designed, Chippendale table. Even if he survived, he knew his heart would be broken by this destruction. Then he saw something far worse.

Brenda and Meredith were dead in the kitchen, lying in pools of blood, their mouths gaping. That they had died here seemed shockingly odd, since there was hardly a trace of damage in the kitchen, compared to the dining room. One window was broken, and there were bullet holes in the refrigerator and stove. It was almost as if Brenda and Meredith had been killed by accident by armed lunatics who preferred to concentrate their ferociousness on structures rather than people.

Why weren't they entering the house? They just kept firing and firing, almost blindly, without reason.

Covering himself with Kintay's .45, Charles worked his way over to the open doorway that led to the back porch. Then he slammed the door and bolted it, knowing it wouldn't hold up against a determined assault.

Janie Stone had been making her way desperately towards the Manor over three miles of dirt road, ever since her mother and grandmother were killed. Hearing the gunfire when she got close, she sneaked into the woods and hid, terrified, in a gully. Then she forced herself to move in closer. She had been trying to get to her father, and now she was terrified that she wouldn't find him alive. Peeping out at the edge of the clearing, she saw that Carson Manor was encircled by a dozen or more terrorists, all blasting away with their weapons. Her daddy's pickup was parked in the brick courtyard alongside other vehicles presumably belonging to the participants in the marriage encounter. Janie didn't know what to do. She wanted to get to her daddy, but how could she dare sticking her head out?

One of the attackers – a skinny long-haired female in jeans and tee shirt – came up close to the house, in a shuffling, zombie-like gait, and clumsily lobbed a grenade. It struck a porch pillar and bounced back at her. She stood stupidly watching the grenade roll back to her feet and explode, destroying her in its roar of smoke and flame.

This incident caused a lull in the firing, as the other attackers just stared like befuddled automatons at the place where their comrade had been standing before the explosion made her 'evaporate'.

Taking advantage of the moment, Janie made a break for the house, yelling, 'Daddy! Daddy!'

The attackers were 'turned on' again by the moving target, and started shooting at her. She dived behind a pile of firewood – a great protective heap of stacked logs. This seemed to dumbfound those who were shooting at her. They appeared not to be able to figure out how simply to go around and get her from behind. They just kept shooting bullets into the logs. Some of their weapons were running out of ammunition, but they still kept squeezing the triggers.

Janie cowered, scared to move or call out again. She had no idea why the attackers all seemed incredibly dumb and slow – like the 'walking dead' she had seen in a movie on the Walshes' TV – but if they heard her voice they might think to come around the side of the log pile.

But because the parlour windows were all shot out, and because of the lull in the firing, George Stone had heard his daughter yelling for him when she had first made her break. He crawled through the demolished interior of the house till he found Charles Walsh in the kitchen, trying to push the huge, heavy refrigerator against the door. 'Doctor Chuck . . . please . . . gotta have the .45,' George said. 'Janie's out there.'

'Where? How do you know?' Charles blurted.

'She was crying out for me. I stuck my head up and saw her duck behind the log pile.'

Charles rummaged in a drawer and came up with a large meat cleaver. 'Take this,' he said. 'We'll both go.'

'No. Gimme the gun,' George protested. 'I'll go alone. If you come with me, it'll leave the door unprotected.'

Reluctantly, he handed the .45 to George Stone. They peeked around the window sashes. There didn't seem to be any attackers on the back porch or in too close to the back of the house. George sneaked out the door while Charles stationed himself there with the meat cleaver.

Soon as the attackers spotted George, they started firing in his direction – but their aim was so bad that he stood a greater chance of getting hit by moving – and that's what he had to do. Bullets whizzing all around him, he dashed back to the woods, skirting the log pile and diving on his face, rolling for cover. This put him almost in the same place Janie had been before she made her break. From there, when the firing died down a bit, George ran as hard as he could for the log pile – putting its height and thickness between himself and the terrorists who were still firing.

'Daddy! Daddy!' Janie cried as he dived in beside her and held her momentarily in his arms. But he couldn't keep still. He had to keep the apparently slow-witted attackers constantly guessing and trying to react. 'Come on, honey!' he shouted, pulling his daughter by her hand.

They ran to the side, then cut sharply for the back porch. They made thirty feet before any shots rang in their direction. Then, while chips were flying out of the steps, they dashed for the door and Charles Walsh flung it open. George pushed Janie in ahead of him. Then he turned and pointed the .45, squeezing off two quick rounds. A bright red hole appeared in the forehead of the nearest terrorist. George watched his target go down, then swung the .45, looking for someone else to shoot.

'Come on! Get *in* here!' Charles Walsh yelled.

George fired at another terrorist, but his shot went wide. Then he whirled and started to step through the door. A loud twang rang out – distinctive from the sound of bullets exploding and ricocheting – and George grunted and fell forward, plummeting face downward across the threshold. Charles Walsh hurriedly dragged him the rest of the way in, then slammed and bolted the door. He saw that a shiny steel bolt was stuck into George's shoulder blade. From what he had seen on the television news, he had little doubt that the shaft was filled with poison – probably rattlesnake venom. He pulled the crossbow bolt out, hoping to be quick enough to prevent a huge dose of the poison from entering the bloodstream. George rolled on to his side against the stove and lay there groaning. Janie hugged him and cried, babbling about her mother and grandmother being killed.

George's mad dash had brought a new hail of gunfire against the people in the house. They cowered behind whatever protection they could find as slugs ripped into furniture and fixtures.

Charles crawled out of the kitchen, then darted upstairs to his bedroom to get his doctor's bag. In it he had antivenin, a medicine he had kept in constant supply since taking up residency in snake-handler country. By the time he came creeping back down the stairs, the latest stage of the fusillade was subsiding. It dwindled to scattered shots. Then it stopped completely.

As if on cue, the telephone started to ring – or maybe it had been ringing before, Charles thought, but nobody had been able to hear it. He crouched and started to work his way to it.

Because of all the shattered windows, the sound of the phone ringing carried outside with crystal clarity. One of the terrorists standing in the yard, near the side of the house, slowly drew a long, sharp bayonet from a sheath.

A pimpled young man with a scraggly beard and dull, dead, yellowish eyes, he moved stiffly but determinedly to the place where telephone and power lines had been strung to the Manor from a nearby pole. With his bayonet, he started slicing the wires.

Sparks flew suddenly – accompanied by screams and sizzles – and the terrorist's body jerked and danced as he was being electrocuted. Finally his clothes caught fire, and he fell to the ground and lay still, in a fetal position, slowly burning.

All power to the Manor had now been cut off. The phone stopped ringing before Charles could crawl to it and pick it up. Dragging his doctor's bag, he crawled back to the kitchen, knelt over George Stone, and injected him with a powerful dose of antivenin. While he was sterilizing and bandaging George's wound, Mark Pearson came crawling in from the parlour.

'We have to get ready to withstand a follow-up assault,' Mark whispered urgently. 'There might not be any time to waste. If the terrorists come at us in a wave – firing their weapons concertedly and tossing grenades through the windows – nothing can stop them from over-running the place and killing us all.'

'Wonder why they haven't done it already,' Charles said.

'It's beyond me,' Mark replied. 'They act sort of like they're all in a daze.'

Charles nodded his head slowly, in baffled agreement. Certainly Kintay had appeared groggy and not in complete control of his faculties before he passed out – but that might be explained if he had been injured in a crash-landing of the Boeing 747. The way he had acted was consistent with the type of behaviour exhibited by persons who were brain-damaged. But it was difficult to see how all of his comrades could have been injured in exactly the same way. If they were *all* in the same condition – each and every one in a state of semi-shock and partial mental deterioration – what in the world could have caused it?

'Where's the strongest place in the house?' Mark Pearson asked.

'The basement,' Charles said without hesitation. 'It was built as a place for shelter in the old days in case of Indian attack. There's a trapdoor in the floor of the pantry. It can be barred once you're down there.'

'We'll make that our place of last resort,' said Mark. 'I'll start trying to get everybody organized.'

He crawled from person to person in the demolished house, rallying the survivors of the attack and assigning them tasks. He had been in the army in the mid-seventies, had received intensive infantry training, but had no actual combat experience since – to his great relief at the time – the United States had pulled out of Vietnam before he could be sent over. In the present situation he was acting braver and more competent than he felt, and he found that doing so helped subdue his fear.

To Mark's chagrin, Sanford Berman was too drunk to help out. He had swilled almost one-third of a fifth of bourbon. With disgust, Mark poured the rest of it down the sink. Sanford's slurred babbling might be dangerous – it could attract the attention of the terrorists and jolt them out of the lethargic but still ominous state into which they seemed to have regressed. Joan was crying softly, huddled in a corner, while her husband ranted that if he was going to die he didn't want to be sober. It was impossible to quiet Sanford, so in the end Mark held him down while Dr Anita Walsh gave him an injection of Demerol to knock him out.

All of the people were scared – some to the point of near hysteria. But Mark was able to calm them enough to gain their cooperation. They crept from room to room, gathering weapons and supplies, trying not to stumble or bump anything or step on a shard of broken glass –

because any sudden loud noise might provoke another outburst of gunfire.

They took turns watching the windows in case an onslaught should come while they were unprepared. And they kept carrying the things they would need down into the basement to make it into a stronghold. Candles. Lanterns. A radio. Food and drink. A Coleman stove. This would be their retreat in case the rest of the house was over-run. The basement had no windows. It was constructed of quarried stone with stout oak beams and trusses to support the upper storeys. It had only one access point – the heavy trapdoor and wooden stairs leading down from the pantry.

Still, it would not be a perfectly safe sanctuary. If the outer defences were breached and the terrorists poured into the house, they could blow the oaken door apart with grenades – something the Indians didn't have in the old days. Then they could toss more grenades down the stairs. The solid confinement of the stone walls would provide enormous concussion. Whoever happened to be down there wouldn't stand a chance. If they didn't die from the grenade blasts, they would be easily finished off by machine gun bursts.

Mark Pearson clung to a vague hope that the terrorists would not be of a mind to carry out such tactics. So far, for some reason, they hadn't acted in an organized, concerted fashion. Perhaps they would continue not to do so.

While Mark was supervising the defensive measures, he noticed the way Heather was looking at him when they passed each other in the midst of some chore, or whenever their eyes happened to meet. She was proud of him once again. Sensing this, he kissed her at one point – a hasty kiss of reassurance – letting her know he was there to protect her.

Funny. For the moment it was almost as if he was in

love with her again, now that he had been forced into a situation in which he, by virtue of his courage and resourcefulness, could feel more needed by her than he had felt in a long time.

20

The FBI helicopters landed at the Charlottesville Airport at 7:35. They didn't get airborne again till almost 8.00 P.M. The command chopper was carrying ten SWAT commandos plus Jim Spencer and Sam Bernardi. The other three choppers were carrying ten SWAT commandos apiece. They flew in close formation to the approximate area where radar contact had been lost with the Boeing 747, one hundred miles northwest of Charlottesville. Then they split off in four quadrants, flying in concentric circles, trying to spot the downed aircraft.

'We're gonna be lucky if we find it tonight,' Bernardi said to Spencer. 'In a half hour we'll lose light. We'll have to head back.'

'Warner and Rice wouldn't have wanted to crash in those mountain forests if they could help it,' said Spencer. 'They'd have tried to look for *some* open space. Let's hope they found it.'

'Not likely,' said Bernardi, looking down at the seemingly impenetrable foliage. From the air, the closely clustered treetops merged into a solid rumpled-green quilt.

'We have to keep hunting till it gets too dark to see anything down there,' Spencer said grimly, exhaling cigarette smoke through his mouth and nostrils. 'We can't afford to lose whatever chance we may have of putting a lid on this thing.'

Bernardi blinked, but other than that his dark-complected face remained expressionless. He wondered to himself: if by some quirk any terrorists or hostages had

144

survived whatever had happened to the 747, how did Jim Spencer imagine that he could cover up the details of the oxygen-deprivation scheme?

The helicopter working the southwest quadrant of the search area spotted the wreckage at 8:45, when the sun had almost sunk behind a ridge of the mountains. 'I see part of the fuselage and a broken-off wing,' the pilot radioed to Jim Spencer. 'Looks like they tried to use a section of gas company right-of-way to force land.' The pilot transmitted the coordinates of the wreckage to the other chopper pilots. Then all four of the choppers converged and hovered over the crash site.

'I don't see any movement down there,' Spencer said. 'We'll go down first. The other three choppers can fan out and cover us.'

Coming down, they saw that most of the right-of-way hadn't been quite broad enough to take the wingspan of the 747. There were great gouges in the level stretch of the grassy tract where the landing gear of the huge jetliner had first struck – then some bouncing, lopsided furrows going up the side of the long hill towards the crest. Both wings had shorn off along the way – probably slowing the approach – but also causing the plane to veer sharply sideways. Part of one wing was lying flat in the right-of-way, and the other wing was leaning in the boughs of a tree. The body of the plane was crashed at about a thirty-degree angle into the woods, with a major part of the tail section protruding, in the clear.

'Hell of a makeshift runway,' Spencer said unemotionally.

Shaking his head in sympathy for the pilots of the 747, Sam Bernardi said, 'They did a good job of trying to improvise. Luck was almost on their side. Looks like the main fuselage is largely intact. There might even be survivors.'

Spencer said nothing to bolster Bernardi's optimism, and the silence reinforced Bernardi's impression that Jim Spencer wasn't exactly praying that any of the terrorists or hostages would still be alive.

The command chopper landed without incident, the SWAT commandos fanning out and advancing in combat squad fashion upon the wrecked aircraft. No shots rang out. The area seemed deserted. The hovering assault choppers swept the perimeter with the muzzles of their mounted machine guns as the squad on the ground moved in, encountering no resistance.

Spencer and Bernardi, both armed with .45 automatics, saw that anyone in the cockpit would probably have been killed. The nose of the plane had ploughed into a tall sycamore, splintering the fat trunk and sending the remains of the tree crashing down, smashing through the cowling.

The main hatch of the wingless plane was gaping wide open. On the ground beneath the hatch – a twenty-foot drop – was a scattered heap of canvas money bags from the Manhattan National Bank. Some of the bags leaked greenbacks which were being blown away into the woods. Up close, bloodstains and muddy boot prints could be seen on the money bags. It looked to Spencer and Bernardi as if the thick bundles of cash had been used to cushion the jump from the hatch to the ground for people escaping from the plane – then they had strolled away as if the money no longer meant anything to them.

Spencer yelled, 'This is the FBI! You are surrounded! Drop your weapons and come out with your hands up!'

He expected no response and got none.

On his orders, two SWAT commandos were boosted up into the gaping hatch. Weapons at the ready, they glanced left into the crushed cockpit, then went in the other direction to secure the passenger areas. Still, no shots rang out. After a few minutes, one of the SWAT men reappeared. He had a funny look on his face. 'Come on up, Commander Spencer,' he said. 'You're not gonna believe this.'

'Is everything okay up there?'

'Yeah. Well . . . sort of.'

Spencer had a walkie-talkie man radio the three hovering choppers to land and have their teams of commandos spread out and do a quick search of the surrounding woods. Meantime, a nylon rope ladder was rigged in the hatch, and Spencer and Bernardi entered the plane. They worked their way down the centre aisle, oxygen masks dangling at nearly every seat. Shorn tree branches were poking through some of the windows. Shredded foliage, broken glass, and assorted articles of military equipment were scattered everywhere.

They saw the hole blown in the fuselage by the exploding grenade. Fred Coogan's body was in the aisle, riddled with bullets. There was a sticky-sweet smell of coagulated blood.

Colonel Chu was dead, sprawled in one of the seats, still wearing an oxygen mask, still cupping gory fingers over the gaping abdominal wound inflicted by Fred Coogan's Urban Slasher.

A couple of seats away, there was a cleancut, square-jawed young man, totally naked, his dark three-piece suit strewn near his feet. He was masturbating absentmindedly, smiling at Spencer and Bernardi and the two SWAT commandos as if his behaviour was not only socially acceptable but commendable.

'Ugh!' said Spencer. 'Maybe we ought to put the poor bastard out of his misery.'

'Wait a minute,' said Bernardi. 'Obviously that was his suit there on the floor. Looks like he was a hostage, not a terrorist.'

'Does it matter?' said Spencer. 'Most of his brain-cells

147

have been killed by lack of oxygen. He's no good to anybody anymore.'

Oblivious to the fact that his own fate was being discussed, the naked young man continued to masturbate. Spencer was utterly disgusted by the spectacle. He fingered his .45, wishing he could use it.

Just then, there was a groan from the direction of the cockpit. Spencer turned, and with a sudden snarl the naked young man, his erection hard still, leapt at Spencer, trying to get his hands around Spencer's throat. The FBI man stepped back and squeezed the trigger of his .45, blowing half of the naked man's head away. They all stared at the body lying in shards of glass. Then they heard another groan from the cockpit. Spencer whirled and snapped at the two SWAT commandos: 'Didn't you check up there to see if anybody was still alive?'

'Commander,' said one of the men, 'it didn't seem like there *could* be. There was a woman on the floor, shot in the head, and the pilot and copilot were both crushed under that big tree. Neither one was moving.'

Spencer headed back up the aisle with the other men following. They pushed their way into the cockpit, past Elizabeth Stoddard's dead body. 'Warner! Rice?' Spencer called out. He peered through the wreckage and the foliage but he couldn't get in far enough to make out who was doing the groaning.

'Spencer . . . is that you?' Larry Warner managed to mumble.

'Yeah! Hang in there, Larry! We'll get you out!' Spencer shouted.

They had to use an acetylene torch and a hydraulic jack from one of the helicopters to burn twisted metal and pry the massive tree away from the bodies of the pilot and copilot. Dave Rice was dead, impaled by a splintered branch a good three inches in diameter. Larry Warner had been pinned in the wreckage in such a way that he had narrowly avoided being crushed to death. Both his legs seemed to be broken, he probably had a few cracked ribs, and possibly some more serious internal injuries. However, before he was given an injection of morphine to ease his pain, he was able to tell Jim Spencer everything he knew about the disaster – the explosion followed by rapid decompression, the burning wing, and the forced landing after being in the air too long to prevent brain damage to the passengers without functional oxygen masks.

'Lucky in a way,' Sam Bernardi said to Jim Spencer, 'that the burning wing got shorn off, or else the whole plane would've exploded.'

'Which would've solved all our problems,' Spencer pointed out. 'All we'd have had to do was put the pieces in body bags.'

'And Warner would be dead, too. You consider that an acceptable price to pay?'

Spencer smiled wryly, the way a realist smiles at an idealist. 'Warner knew the risks before he accepted the mission. He and Rice and I gave the director our word that we'd do whatever was necessary to avoid embarrassment to the Bureau.'

Bernardi felt uncomfortable, even embarrassed, being the devil's advocate. Usually he was the hard, cynical stoic who went along with the programme. 'How about the hostages?' he heard himself saying. '*They* didn't know all the risks.'

'But,' said Spencer, 'they weren't in a position to be told. We did what we thought they would have wanted us to do. We were trying to save their lives. We can't take any of the blame for their condition as it stands right now. The public outcry would destroy the Bureau. It'd do what Watergate did to the CIA – weakened their credibility so much it damned near put them out of business.'

Bernardi eyed Spencer incredulously. 'When you say we can't take any of the blame . . . surely you don't mean – ' He didn't finish his sentence, but both he and Spencer knew that he had almost asked out loud whether Spencer meant to kill the hostages.

Spencer evaded a direct answer to the aborted question. 'I can tell you that I've already made some tough decisions, and I fully intend to implement them, for the good of the Bureau. I'm in command of this operation, and I expect your loyalty and cooperation, Bernardi, if you plan on sticking around for the mop-up.'

'Suppose we *can* save some of the hostages,' Bernardi said, desperately trying to provide Spencer with an alternative to going off the deep end. 'We can give out a news release blaming the whole thing on the Green Brigade. We can say that they exploded a grenade, forcing the plane to crash-land. We can state that the pilot is okay, but that some of the hostages and terrorists may have suffered brain damage due to the fact that the oxygen supply to the passenger area was disrupted by the explosion.'

'That's a good idea,' said Spencer, mulling it over, lighting up a cigarette.

Bernardi was relieved – and stunned that he had got his point across so easily.

But then Spencer added, 'I mean it's a good idea in case we don't nail them all. With that kind of news release, our asses will be covered if one of the brain-damaged people happens to get away and is picked up by civilian authorities. Good thinking, Bernardi.'

Sam Bernardi just stared, then turned away in defeat and disbelief. Why had he come out here into these mountains? Why hadn't he stayed back at the airport? In his days in Vietnam he hadn't got involved with the dirty work of his combat missions to any greater extent than was required of him. He had flown men in and flown men out. He hadn't squeezed any triggers – that had been done by the gunnery crews on the choppers and the assault troops on the ground. He had never volunteered for anything. He had done what he had to do and that's all. Why was he sticking his neck out now? Spencer was in command. Whatever happened was Spencer's responsibility ethically and morally.

Then why did Bernardi feel that he had to hang in? That he had to do something to prevent unnecessary bloodshed?

Could it be that subconsciously he, the stoic, the apparent cynic, was looking for a chance to atone for some of the things he had condoned and blessed with silence fifteen years ago in the Vietnamese jungles and rice paddies?

21

All of the firing had stopped about an hour ago. Some of the attackers had fired till their guns were empty, but many others still had full clips.

The sun had gone down, but the warm June night was crystal clear. The stars and moon were so bright that the terrorists ringing Carson Manor could be plainly seen when they moved among the shadows of the sycamore and weeping willow trees.

Charles Walsh, Mark and Heather Pearson, and Ben Harris were keeping a lookout from four separate downstairs windows, covering each of the four sides of the house. None of them was very well armed. Mark had the .45 taken from Kintay, with plenty of spare ammunition, but it was not a long-range weapon. Charles, Heather, and Ben had Civil War black-powder antiques – a muzzle-loading Richmond rifle, a Union Navy Colt, and a Confederate revolver – that had been hanging in the Walshes' study. They also each had a knife or a meat cleaver. All of the guards knew that they could do little if the terrorists started blasting away at the house from a distance. Their job was to fend off any attackers who tried, individually or en masse, to break into the house or come up close enough to lob in grenades.

If they were overwhelmed and couldn't man their outposts anymore, they agreed they would run for the trapdoor and pound on it. Someone would unbar it for them. They would scramble down into the basement to take their chances with the rest of the people. Joan Berman. Sophie Harris. Anita Walsh. Andrea Warnak. All able-bodied adults even if they were frightened, worried, and grief-stricken. There were some other adults down there who weren't so able-bodied. George Stone, feverish and delirious, was lying on an old sofa with Janie hovering anxiously over him. Sanford Berman was sprawled on an aluminum chaise longue with busted webbing; he was snoring heavily, stinking of bourbon. General Kintay was still tied and gagged, lying on a mat on the hard-packed dirt floor.

The portable radio in the basement was tuned to an all-news station. The survivors of the terrorist attack were hoping that there would be a special bulletin telling them that the authorities were aware that the Green Brigade plane had come down in this area of the country, and help would be on the way. So far they had heard nothing to this effect. Nothing but ordinary news of ordinary disasters, politics, sports and weather.

Upstairs, at his station near one of the parlour windows, Dr Charles Walsh had another portable radio tuned to the same station. He was listening to it through an earplug. Cradled in his arms was his Richmond rifle of Civil War vintage. The past versus the present. Modern horror was destroying what he cherished and held most dear.

Immersing himself in nostalgia, he had learned to load and shoot the old pistols and the muzzle-loader that he was now using to defend himself. He had shot at nothing but bull's-eye targets and cardboard silhouettes of deer and grizzly bear. He had been too gentle, too squeamish, to shoot at live game. He had only wanted to get a feeling for what it must have been like for the people of a bygone era who had had to depend upon these weapons for survival. It had never occurred to him that he might one day have to kill a human being.

Ironically, so far as Charles knew from his historical research, Carson Manor had never had to withstand an Indian attack; however, when it was first built precautions

153

had been taken with that in mind. Most of the Southeastern tribes had been vanquished by white men's bullets or diseases in the decades before the Manor started to flourish. Now a danger far worse than savage Indians was being faced with weapons competent against arrows and tomahawks.

Looking out across the front lawn of his estate, Charles could see his enemies milling under the trees, going in and out of the moonlit shadows, like ghostly spectres. They didn't seem to have any goal, any purpose. They were evil for evil's sake. And Charles didn't understand why. What had made them that way? Like a primitive man, he felt the mind-wrenching terror of what he could not comprehend.

Basically, he had always been a man of ideas, intrigued by intellectual subtleties and nuances. He was accustomed to dealing abstractly with the mental and emotional problems of his patients. Now he was facing the challenge of becoming a man of action rather than contemplation, so he might help save their lives.

Meantime, Jim Spencer was on his way by helicopter to Richmond, where there was a regional FBI office. There wasn't one in Charlottesville. Spencer had arranged to use the office to keep in touch with the director in Washington and to supervise the composition and dissemination of his news release. Except for Spencer and the pilot, the helicopter was empty.

The other three assault helicopters had been sent back to Charlottesville. One of them was carrying Larry Warner to a hospital. The others were taking the SWAT men to a hangar area where they could camp for the night. At dawn, Spencer would rejoin them. It was too dark now to comb the forests for signs of the terrorists, but come daylight it would be a different story. They could be hunted down and exterminated the way Spencer

154

had dreamed of doing ever since the Green Brigade first began their heinous escapades.

He had decided that any mountain people who might be in danger would have to wait till tomorrow to be rescued. The excuse given to the news media would be that it had got too dark by the time the wreckage of the 747 was located. The real reason was that Spencer wanted to keep the mop-up an FBI operation exclusively if he could help it. He didn't want to ask the local or state cops to try to check on some of the isolated families because if they started poking around they might discover something that could embarrass him or the Bureau. If he could control everything till the end, he might be able to stage and construct a scenario that would take the heat off.

When he arrived at the FBI office in Richmond, he intended to prepare a news release revealing that the jetliner was down and the pilot was safe after a forced landing was made necessary when the terrorists exploded a grenade in the passenger area. Some of the hostages and terrorists were killed in the fracas, and some apparently suffered brain damage due to the fact that the oxygen supply to the passenger area must have been disrupted by the exploding grenade. The news release would not say anything about the FBI mop-up operation that would be launched tomorrow morning. And it would not reveal the exact location where the 747 went down, so that people living in that area would not be panicked, and local lawmen would not be encouraged to meddle.

Heather Pearson was terrified, yet she was proud of her husband and proud of herself for having the courage to stand the first watch with him. She was stationed in the kitchen and Mark was next door in the dining room. Conscientiously heeding his advice, she stayed close enough to the window to observe, but back far enough in the shadows not to be easily picked off. A butcher's knife was in her belt. She kept her hand within easy reach of the big, heavy, Confederate revolver on the sink counter. If she and Mark got out of this alive . . .

She told herself that if anybody got out of it alive it'd be largely thanks to her husband. She felt that he was really showing what he was made of. His manhood had come to the fore in this emergency. He had made everybody do what had to be done even if they were too scared and shook up to think for themselves. Heather had done things that she didn't even know she was capable of doing without going to pieces. The most awful, saddest thing was helping to carry the bloody bodies of Brenda and Meredith Meachum upstairs, laying them on a bed, and covering them with a sheet. It would be unbearable to have to stand and watch in the dining room if the bodies were still in there.

One good thing about the kitchen, it was the closest lookout post to the basement. The pantry was behind Heather's back and to her right. The trapdoor was only about ten feet away. She figured that Mark had put her here on purpose, to try to keep her as safe as possible – and near to him. Maybe it had taken a crisis to make him realize how much he truly cared for her. Maybe he loved her after all. Maybe they would be able to rebuild their life together. If they got out of this alive.

Heather realized that the reason Mark was almost like his old self – even though he was scared and under stress – was that he was doing something valuable, something basic, something he had no trouble believing in. He was fighting for everybody's survival, and he knew he was doing a good job of it. If he hadn't seized the reins, who else would have? Maybe this new sense of his own value would rekindle another kind of spark in him. Maybe when this was over, he'd start believing in himself not only as a man but as an artist.

Or, would he sink back down into despair and self-pity once the adrenaline stopped flowing?

Heather didn't know, but she could see a spark of hope.

Suddenly one of the horses whinnied – startling her because the sound carried so loud and clear through the broken window. She risked leaning forward to peer out towards the corral. Bullet and Lightning were both whinnying, rearing back in fright. They started pawing at the corral posts, trying to kick down the top rail. Then Heather saw what the animals were afraid of. She picked up the Confederate revolver, clenching her hand tightly around the butt. Three terrorists in a close cluster were shuffling slowly towards the corral. One of them emitted a demented snicker.

'What's going on out there?' Mark whispered hoarsely from the dining room.

'The horses!' Heather whispered back. 'They're scared!'

'Are you all right?' Mark wanted to know.

Then the firing started.

Horrendous machine gun bursts.

Heather ducked back, throwing herself on the floor. But they weren't shooting at her. No bullets came her way. They were killing the beautiful palominos.

They kept firing till their weapons started making those stupid, repetitive clicks.

'Heather!' Mark said in a shouted whisper.

She stuck her head up. She saw the horses lying dead in the corral. Even some of the fence rails were splintered, shot to pieces.

'The horses are dead!' she cried. 'They shot Bullet and Lightning!'

'Shhhh!' Mark whispered back.

Heather had forgotten to keep her voice down. Tears rolling down her cheeks, she clutched the revolver, expecting a fusillade to be directed at the house. But nothing happened. Just the guns going click . . . click . . . click . . . click . . .

Mustering the courage to peek out again, she saw the three terrorists who had killed the horses still standing by the corral, still squeezing their triggers on empty chambers, like mindless malevolent automatons. A half dozen more automatons came up behind their backs, from the woods to the right, and stood quietly, just watching. Then Heather realized that these new ones didn't have any weapons. She squinted to make out additional details. Two of them were ladies who appeared to be dressed rather chicly; one was even wearing high-heeled shoes. Another was a man in a business suit. It dawned on Heather that they must have been Green Brigade hostages. She wondered why they would hang around the yard in such close proximity to their former captors. She jumped when they turned slowly, eerily, towards her in the moonlight, eyeing the house with the same vacant hostility that the terrorists exhibited, but lacking the terrorists' weapons.

When the shots fired at the horses had caused Heather to dive on the floor, one of the ex-hostages had stepped on to the back porch. He was now lurking out of Heather's view, between the window and the door. He was a young man with long hair dyed orange and teased into spikes. He was wearing a tight red jumpsuit of a synthetic, shiny fabric. Dried blood caked his nose and his broken, twisted, front teeth.

Unlike most of the other ex-hostages, he was armed. he was carrying the rifle dropped by the terrorist who had electrocuted himself cutting the power lines to the house. He was not carrying the rifle in a military fashion. He was clutching the loosened sling in his hand, letting the weapon dangle, as if it were an interesting item that he

158

had found in the course of his meanderings, but one that he did not know exactly how to use.

He had spotted Heather's face in the window, and he knew that he wanted her. He had always dreamed of screwing a clean, blonde, pretty woman. Now his damaged brain could contemplate nothing else. He leaned the rifle against the porch railing. Ever so quietly, sneakily, and single-mindedly, he unzipped his shiny red jumpsuit and took it off.

How could he grab the woman? She was too far away.

He looked at the sling of the rifle, which to him was like a rope on a stick. He had once seen a dog-catcher use such a stick to grab a mongrel by the neck.

He crouched on the back porch, his erection throbbing as he waited for the woman to come closer to the window so he could grab her with his rope-stick.

The watch was supposed to change in fifteen more minutes, at eleven o'clock. Sophie Harris was torn between wanting the time to come so Ben's turn would end safely, and not wanting the time to come because she was so afraid to go upstairs. She was sitting at the bottom of the basement steps, glancing up at the trapdoor every now and then. A few minutes ago when she had heard the machine gun fire out back she had jumped up, her heart pounding, expecting whoever wasn't shot to be hammering for her to let them in. But then things had quieted down. She hadn't had to unbar the door, but she hadn't been able to stop trembling, worrying about Ben. She had been startled by Anita Walsh's soft, professionally comforting voice: 'Don't worry . . . it must've been just a random outburst. If anything drastic happens up there, they'll surely let us know.'

'But what if they're all dead?' Sophie had sobbed. 'How do we know they weren't all killed by those guns that just went off? They could be lying dead and the terrorists could be coming for us right *now*.'

'No, I don't believe so,' Anita had replied calmly. 'All of those shots came from the back of the house, and our lookouts are posted on four sides. They couldn't all be hit by bullets coming from one direction.'

The simple logic of the explanation had astounded Sophie. She had always felt a warm respect for Dr Anita Walsh, and now her admiration deepened. It awed her that Anita could think logically and clearly in such a terrible situation. But her urge to panic still overcame the logic. She wouldn't stop worrying feverishly about Ben till the fifteen minutes were up and he came down the steps unharmed.

Ever since his retirement, he had been a pest, hanging around her all day long, telling her what to do. He had worked for forty years as an industrial engineer and had formed deep habits. He couldn't stop being a time-study man, an 'efficiency expert' – even when he only had his wife Sophie to practice on. It had got so bad that she had seriously considered divorcing him at this late stage of their lives.

But now she'd love to wake up tomorrow to some normal nit-picking. She longed for what was ordinary. Having coffee and sweet rolls in the morning. Watching the sun come up over the tall buildings that ringed their high-rise apartment. Listening to her husband tell her how she should go about cleaning the oven or ironing a shirt. She guessed she could put up with Ben's nagging through her twilight years if only she would get to share them with him.

Anita Walsh was examining George Stone, who was lying on his side, sedated. When he had first received his wound, his pulse had become irregular, he had become extremely nauseous and dizzy. He had vomited on the kitchen floor while Charles was bandaging him. Now he looked much better, although he was still perspiring profusely, and the flesh around the wound was black and swollen due to ruptured blood vessels. His symptoms were typical reactions to blood-coagulating venom – like that carried by rattlesnakes – as opposed to the nerve-paralyzing venom of cobras.

'Doctor Anita,' Janie Stone said in a weak, forlorn voice. 'Is my father going to die?'

'I don't believe so, honey,' Anita said, hugging Janie to her. 'We think we gave him the antivenin in time. Maybe the crossbow bolt didn't go in deep because your father's back is so heavily muscled. Besides, it happened to strike the shoulder blade. He may have got only a few drops of venom. So far, the antivenin seems to be working.'

Anita knew that if George had been poisoned with neurotoxic venom he'd have been dead already. The antivenin the Walshes kept on hand was good only against the copperheads, rattlers, and cottonmouths they were likely to encounter around here. Luckily for George, hemotoxic venom was more slow-acting than the other kind. The main problem in George's case was that he may have received an enormous quantity of venom instead of only the few drops that Anita had hopefully mentioned. How much would a fanatic put into his crossbow bolts? Would he load a lot into a few bolts, or would he stretch it to cover a large inventory of poisonous shafts?

'How does antivenin work?' Janie asked timidly.

'It's like a vaccination,' Anita explained. 'A horse can be made immune to snake poison by injecting it with stronger and stronger doses, over a period of time. Then the horse's blood is used to make antevenin to cure humans.'

'I never heard of antevenin,' said Janie. 'The people in

my church would never use it. We believe in healing through prayer.'

'Sit by your daddy and pray for him, Janie,' Anita said, caressing the child's head.

Shocked and grieving over what she imagined must have happened to her husband, Andrea Warnak was slumped in an aluminium lawn chair in a dusty, dingy corner of the basement. She knew in her heart that her husband was dead, and she was to blame.

Earlier today, in their room when they were getting dressed for dinner, Andrea and Harvey had had an argument. He had accused her of flirting with Dr Charles Walsh, and she had denied it, telling him, 'I don't see why it should matter to you anyway. You've been trying to drive me away from you ever since I had my operation.'

The truth was that she *had* been flirting. It wasn't that she wanted anything to happen between her and Charles – she just wanted to see if she could make him like her. She needed to feel that some other man might find her appealing even if her husband didn't.

When she had been convalescing from the brain operation that almost killed her, she had had no emotional resources left to deal with her husband's rejection of her. The loss of his love at a time like that would have utterly devastated her. Rather than face the possibility, she at first had pretended that it did not exist. Then, as she had slowly recovered her physical health over the long months, she had got strong enough to fight on the emotional battlefield.

But in the end, constantly going up against Harvey's wall of anger, spite, and alienation had worn her down. She had gradually begun to accept the idea that her marriage might not last, and perhaps didn't deserve to. Her illness might have exposed a fatal flaw, a crack in the seam, that wouldn't have been apparent under less stressful circumstances.

She had found herself looking at Harvey with a more critical eye. She had found herself looking at other men, comparing them to her husband, and imagining their good points to outweigh his.

To Andrea, a man like Charles Walsh was everything that her husband wasn't – literate, intellectual, genteel. But when Harvey had accused her of flirting with Charles, she had reacted with anger and defensiveness. 'Are you implying that I have a crush on our psychiatrist? Don't be absurd!'

She had made no attempt to reach out to her husband and reassure him, as they were taught to do in their counselling sessions. Instead, to goad him further, with haughty intensity she had continued her flirting over dinner and afterwards in the parlour. She blamed herself for driving him to his fate. It was because of her that Harvey had gone out for a walk by himself, probably half high on sherry and unable to defend himself even if he had a chance. If it hadn't been for her, he'd still be here. He'd still be safe.

It seemed so far away now . . . like a guilty dream. It was hard for her to believe that just a few hours ago she and her husband had been having dinner and cocktails with everybody else, smooth people in suits and evening dresses, playing spiteful emotional games with one another. Now everyone was in jeans and slacks, dirty and bloodstained. Everybody was wallowing in guilt, fear, grief, and anxiety. And Harvey was missing . . . probably dead. Andrea would dearly love to have him back with her to try to make the most of their lives, whether they stayed together or not.

Considering the group of weary, frightened people clustered with her in the smoky, gritty glow of the kerosene lamps placed around the basement, she guessed that she wasn't the only one who would like to turn the clock back. Compared with the elemental struggle for survival they were all immersed in now, the problems that had brought each couple here seemed tame and manageable.

Andrea looked up as Anita Walsh finished pouring two cups of coffee from the pot on the Coleman stove and brought one over to her. 'Hot coffee to keep you alert,' Anita said. 'Five more minutes and we take our turn on watch.'

'Thank you,' Andrea said, feigning gratefulness, although the mere idea of going upstairs filled her with so much adrenaline that she certainly wouldn't need caffeine to keep her awake.

'How are you doing, dear?' Anita inquired solicitously.

'All right . . . I'm hanging in . . . I'll make it,' Andrea answered grimly.

'Try to be optimistic about Harvey. If he saw that this place was surrounded, he may have ducked back into the woods. He may have taken shelter somewhere . . . he may even be going for help.'

'That's what I've told myself,' Andrea lied. Intuitively she knew that Harvey wasn't coming back. She wished that Anita Walsh would just go away and leave her alone. Alone with her guilt and her dread.

She got her wish.

Sanford Berman groaned, and Anita went to have a look at him. 'The Demerol is wearing off,' she told Joan, who was sitting on a chair beside the chaise longue. 'He's waking up. He'll have an awful headache and a sick stomach, but otherwise he should be all right.'

'Unless he gets his hands on another bottle,' Joan whispered.

'I'm afraid that he can't,' Anita said. 'All the bottles were broken but the one he grabbed. The liquor cabinet got a good strafing after that.'

'What can I do for him?' Joan asked wearily.

'Try to get him to take lots of black coffee. If he can revitalize himself, he might as well pull his weight around here.'

Sanford opened his bloodshot eyes. In the dim orange glow of the lanterns, he resembled a pasty-skinned, red-headed ogre in a carnival funhouse. Joan knelt beside him, cradling his head in her arms to help him sit up. 'Honey . . . you're all right . . . I'm getting you some coffee,' she crooned.

'What happened? Where are we?' he muttered hoarsely. Then as remembrance dawned on him, he moaned, 'Oh, shit . . . was anybody shot?'

'Shhh!' Sophie Harris hissed. She had jumped up and was pointing at the radio which was sitting on an old three-legged stool. 'They're talking about the Green Brigade! They know that the plane never made it to Cuba!'

A hush fell over everyone in the basement as they strained not to miss a word of the broadcast.

The naked ex-hostage with the spiky orange hair still had a powerful erection. His rope-stick in his right hand, he was standing on the back porch, pressing his back flat against the wall between the window and the door. When he leaned slightly forward, he could see out of the corner of his left eye whether the pretty blonde head was close enough to the broken-out window for him to drop the noose of the rope-stick around her neck. So far she was staying too far back in the semi-darkness. It was driving him to a lustful frenzy. His testicles were aching to unload. His throbbing penis wanted to dive and plunge inside her, tearing her apart. His mind and his penis were one with this sweet, violent, instinctive craving.

His rope-stick . . .

His rope-stick would capture her like a mongrel, like a bitch in heat, if only she would come a bit closer . . .

22

Mark Pearson said, 'That explains why the hostages are out there along with the terrorists. They're all brain-damaged. I guess the hostages could be almost as dangerous to us as the terrorists now.'

Heather brought Mark a cup of black coffee and handed it to him. The watch had changed, and the people who had been downstairs were now upstairs, and vice versa, except for George and Janie Stone, Sanford Berman, and of course – Kintay.

Over his portable radio with earplug, Charles Walsh had heard the special news bulletin – a mixture of facts and lies planted by the FBI man Jim Spencer – and had relayed the information to the members of his watch. 'You're absolutely right,' Charles said to Mark. 'I suspected that Kintay had suffered some profound injury of the neocortex, and that radio report confirmed my worst fears.'

'What do you mean?' Sanford Berman asked, his hung-over voice hoarse and quavering.

Heather sat beside Mark on a basement step at the foot of the stairs. She was so glad to be off duty. Seeing the palominos killed had unnerved her. She had started to hear funny noises – noises that probably weren't even there. Just before Andrea had relieved her, she had imagined she might have heard a coughing sound. She had leaned forward as far as she dared, and had spotted nothing human – or subhuman – in the back yard. She had peered sideways to check out the porch, but she wasn't about to get her face too close to the windowsill. She hadn't been able to see the outside wall, but she had seen enough to be convinced that it wasn't worth sticking her neck out any farther. If somebody or something was flattened against that wall, he'd have done his damage before now.

'When there's oxygen deprivation,' Charles Walsh explained, 'the part of the human brain that suffers worst is the most advanced part – the neocortex. It's the seat of complex logic and subtle reasoning. It has a lot to do with what makes us sensitive humans. When it is damaged, all sorts of unpredictable behaviour regressions can result.'

'Oh my God!' Ben Harris exclaimed. 'We're dealing with mindless monsters, and we're surrounded by fifty or sixty of them!'

'More specifically, I'd say we're dealing with the reptile complex,' said Charles. 'The things Janie had to say about the attack on her, coupled with my observations of Kintay, had me thinking in that direction. But until I heard the news bulletin it was difficult to see how that type of brain damage could've happened to so many people simultaneously.'

'Oh, shit! Brain damage!' Sanford Berman growled. He bounced to his feet and paced around, red-faced and fuming. Charles stared at him, dismayed. Apparently his hangover wasn't going to keep him sick and sheepish. He was the type who'd rather be mad at the world than disgusted with himself. As long as he could go on ranting and raving, he might more easily forget his fear and his nerve-racking need for more liquor.

'What is this about the reptile complex?' asked Mark Pearson.

'Highbrow bullshit!' scoffed Sanford Berman.

Ignoring him, Charles said, 'You have to understand how the human brain evolved. The most primitive part, inherited from our reptile ancestors, has remained intact inside us without developing. Sections were added on as evolution progressed to mammals and ultimately to man.

167

The limbic system, which began to show up in early mammals, is the seat of our capacity for nurturing and caring about others – qualities that are utterly lacking in reptiles. The neocortex was the last part of our brains to evolve, giving us our power to discriminate and reason. When it loses its control over the reptile complex, we become creatures devoid of ethics and morality.'

'I don't believe in evolution and all that crap!' shouted Sanford Berman. 'Those goddamned terrorists were already brain-damaged. Now they're just worse, that's all.'

'Some people look at it this way,' Charles said mildly. 'Who was the tempter in the Garden of Eden? The serpent. The reptile. In other words, the reptilian side of *man* – that's who the devil was.'

'Bullshit!' said Sanford. 'I don't believe in what you're saying, any more than I believe in a *real* devil with horns and a tail!'

'The reptile complex is the seat of deception and aggression,' Charles said sadly but forcefully. 'The people who have us trapped here are like primitive beasts, driven by the urge to rape or kill or eat – to gratify whatever impulse they may feel at any given moment.'

'But they seem to still possess some rudimentary intelligence,' said Mark Pearson.

'Yes,' Charles agreed. 'That's because their brains have gaps, or blocks of cells whose synapses were randomly killed off by the lack of sufficient oxygen. It's hard to say just what kind of aberrant behaviour may come to the fore as the result of some specific type of brain damage.'

'Ironic that they've become snakes, just like their insignia,' said Ben Harris.

'Grandma was right,' Janie Stone murmured, her voice so low that nobody heard her. She prayed harder for her daddy, realizing that it had taken a human snake to put venom into him, instead of one of the ones from the serpent box.

'In a way,' said Charles, 'our enemies outside this house are evolutionary throwbacks. They lack the human compassion that resides in the neocortex. Their behaviour is akin to the behaviour of lizards.'

Heather shuddered. 'How so?' she asked, cowering closer to Mark.

'Lizards are clever, patient, and singleminded about stalking, ambushing, and devouring their victims. They sometimes attack in swarms if they find a helpless prey, but they don't usually cooperate in the truest, most meaningful sense.'

'That's why they haven't organized to overrun us,' said Mark. 'They're content to wait for us to come out of our hole.'

'Right,' said Charles. 'Now that we understand that for sure, we may be able to work it to our advantage.'

'I don't want to understand the damned creeps!' snapped Sanford Berman. 'I just want to figure a way to get the hell out of here!'

'Understanding one's enemy is the first rule of survival,' Charles went one, thinking aloud. 'In a way, our enemy is ourselves . . . the part of ourselves responsible for the dichotomy of good and evil inside every man. I've always thought it was sort of an evolutionary blunder that prevented the newer parts of our brains from dominating the older, more savage parts. In these days of nuclear weapons, our primitive impulses can wreak such horrible havoc in the world that we may not survive as a species.'

'I'll worry later about surviving as a species,' said Sanford Berman. 'Right now I just want to survive as a person.'

As she stood by the kitchen window nervously observing the ominous figures moving around the back yard, Andrea

Warnak could not stop thinking about the news report and its implications, which had been explained to her and Sophie Harris and Joan Berman by Anita Walsh, before they went on watch. Her mind was a jumble of confused, frightening thoughts about what those 'mindless beasts' might have done to her husband, and what might have happened to her if her brain operation a year and a half ago hadn't turned out successfully. Perhaps the tumour, or the laser beam that had been used to vaporize it, might have destroyed enough of her mental faculties to make her into a creature similar to the ones who were out there now trying to get her.

Her tumour had been the size of a plum, growing on her left optic nerve, wrapping itself around other nerves and arteries. When it was diagnosed by a CAT scan, it had already caused some loss of vision in her left eye, and was pressing on her right optic nerve. It had been explained to her and Harvey that surgery deep in the eye socket where the optic nerve led to the brain was the most dangerous and complicated kind of neurosurgery. A surgical laser could easily wreak greater damage than it was trying to combat. Weighing all these facts, she had consented to letting the surgeons open her skull and try to burn out, with utmost delicacy and precision, a plum-sized lump lodged right between her eyes.

She reminded herself that she had been brave then, and she must be brave now. According to Dr Anita Walsh, the creatures outside weren't likely to attack in an organized, methodical way. They were like lizards watching a mousehole. They knew what they wanted, but not exactly how to get at it. Their brains were damaged; their thinking was impaired. The mental functions they were still capable of were very primitive, very basic, unable to encompass subtle strategical concepts. That was why first watch had seen only one random destructive incident: the slaughter of the two horses. Andrea told herself that nothing worse was likely to happen on second watch.

Down in the basement, Mark Pearson was pushing a similar viewpoint. 'As I see it, the main thing is making it through the night.. Come daylight this part of the country will probably be swarming with lawmen. If we can sit tight and protect ourselves the way we have been doing, we're bound to be rescued.'

'Oh, yeah?' Sanford Berman jeered. 'If the authorities are so much on the ball,, why didn't they say a word about where they found the plane? I don't trust them. I don't think we should depend on anybody to come and save us. I'm for getting the hell out of here soon as we can come up with a plan.'

'Me, too,' said Ben Harris. 'We might stand a good chance. Some of the terrorists have empty guns now.'

'Some but not all,' said Mark. 'Unfortunately, they didn't all get carried away enough to use up their ammo.'

'I told you they're like lizards,' said Charles Walsh. 'I don't think they'll come in for us, they'll wait for us to come to them. If we panic, we'll be like mice running out of a hole right into the lizards' jaws.'

'Bullshit!' said Sanford Berman. 'Your theory might not be right even though you make it sound so logical. You're an egghead – a highbrow – you try to reason everything out. You're hung up on motives and psychology and all that crap. But while you're busy thinking and wondering, the world goes on reacting. Those things out there don't behave according to reason. What reason did they have for gunning down your horses, for Christ's sake?'

'That's right,' said Ben Harris. 'We don't really know what they're liable to do next. I feel more scared of them now, knowing their brains are damaged, than I felt before. At least before I could entertain the hope that if

171

we gave their leader Kintay back to them they might leave us alone. Now it seems like there's no way of dealing with them if worse comes to worst.'

'Christ, I need a drink,' Sanford Berman moaned, rubbing his tired, bloodshot eyes. 'Now that I've taken the plunge, I might as well have one.' He looked pleadingly at Charles Walsh. 'Just a hair of the dog. Something to straighten me up. Coffee alone won't do it.'

'There's nothing left,' said Charles. 'The liquor cabinet was shot up.'

'I thought maybe Joan was lying to me about that,' Sanford said hopefully.

'I'm afraid not,' Charles told him. 'You should be glad. You're better off sober in a situation like this.'

'That's debatable,' Sanford growled. 'For your information, I can stop drinking again if I survive this, but right now, by God, I doubt if I can make it without something strong enough to settle my nerves.'

Underneath his veneer of bravado and belligerence, Sanford was badly shaken by the realization that even when he had tried to scare himself by thinking about his suicide attempt in the jail cell in Nashville, it hadn't been enough of a boogeyman to keep him from going for that bottle of bourbon and swilling it while the house was under fire. The threat of succumbing to his self-destructive impulses had kept him sober for over a year – why hadn't it worked now? He believed it was because he was more afraid of being butchered by those mindless creatures outside than he was of dying by his own hand. It even occurred to him that this was the kind of shrewd insight that Charles Walsh would love to pick apart and examine, but damned if he ever intended to tell Charles about it.

Suddenly, Andrea heard a scraping, shuffling noise coming from the back porch. Her heart leapt into her throat. She clutched the Confederate revolver tightly in her hand. Leaning forward a bit, over the sink counter, she peered in the direction of the noise – but it was out of her view. Then it happened again – a slow, scraping shuffle – and it dawned on her that someone could be sneaking up the side steps, ready to lob in a grenade. She trembled, picturing herself blown to pieces in a terrible instant. She glanced at the trapdoor. She could bang on it for help, but by the time anyone opened it the grenade that she imagined would already have gone off and she'd be dead.

Again she heard the scraping sound.

Maybe it was some nocturnal animal. Maybe she needn't be so scared. A groundhog or a weasel might have come up on to the back porch.

She waited, holding her breath, the revolver heavy in her hand. The seconds ticked by like the ticking of her own mortality. Nothing happened. Maybe it had been her mind playing tricks on her. Maybe the wind was blowing something on the porch. Maybe if it had been an animal prowling around, it had now gone away.

The scraping sound came again.

She couldn't stay here wondering about it. Her watch had over an hour yet to run. She'd be a gibbering wreck if she had to spend all that time in fear and suspense.

She forced herself to stick her neck out farther and have a quick but really good look, to reassure herself that the grenade she had pictured was not about to be lobbed in on her.

Snap! The rifle sling dropped over her head – then it was jerked and twisted, cutting off her scream. She felt the twisting barrel grinding the side of her face, the sling cutting into her soft neck, silencing the larynx by crushing it shut. With super strength – the kind that victims of neocortical and limbic damage often possess – the naked man with the orange spiky hair dragged Andrea bodily up and out of the broken window, ripping her clothes and flesh on sharp jagged bits of remaining glass. The Confederate revolver dropped out of her hand with a loud metallic clatter in the bowl of the sink. Her hips and legs slammed on to the iron porch railing, then spragged and thudded on to the stones as the naked man continued dragging and strangling her with his 'rope-stick' down the steps and across the yard.

By that time – having heard Andrea's choked-off scream – Sophie Harris had come running from the dining room and was staring out the back window, forgetting to hang back in the shadows. In her hand was Kintay's .45, but she didn't know what to do with it. In the moonlight, she could see Andrea flopping and kicking, and the naked wild man dragging her and ripping at her clothes as he crouched over her with his huge erection. But should Sophie shoot? It seemed too late to save Andrea. And she was afraid that once the .45 went off the terrorists would start shooting at her.

While Sophie was frozen in indecision, Andrea – in her dying throes – had managed to claw at the attacker's testicles. He howled and jerked savagely on his 'rope-stick' – inadvertently catching his finger in the trigger guard – and the rope-stick fired a burst of rounds – blowing away Andrea's face.

This brought an answering fire from a group of terrorists who had been standing by the corral, staring with brutish fascination at the slaughtered horses. The ex-hostage flailed through the air, clutching at the bullets that stitched into his naked torso as if he thought he could pluck them out – then he crumpled in a lifeless heap, nearly cut in two.

Sophie Harris bolted for the trapdoor and pounded on it as hard as she could, yelling, 'Let me in! It's Sophie! Please! Let me in!'

The terrorists were now shooting at the house, on all sides.

When Mark Pearson flung open the trapdoor, Sophie Harris almost bowled him over scrambling down into the basement. She fell into her husband's arms, bawling and babbling about what had happened to Andrea.

Mark Pearson waited to see if Joan Berman and Anita Walsh were also going to desert their posts.

'Bar the door!' Ben Harris shouted. 'Joan and Anita aren't coming! They must be dead!'

'Give them a chance!' barked Charles Walsh.

'We can't *all* hide in the basement!' Mark yelled. 'We've got to know what's happening up there!'

He crawled to the kitchen window, pulled himself up by hanging on to the sink counter, and peeked over the window sill. A bullet chewed into the sill, powdering his face with splinters and mortar dust. He ducked down. But he had seen enough to be sure that the terrorists weren't swarming nearer to the house. They were just peppering away at it, and already their enthusiasm for this activity seemed to be waning. It occurred to Mark that like morons or infants the brain-damaged terrorists had very brief attention spans.

He retrieved the Confederate revolver that Andrea Warnak had dropped into the sink bowl. Then, while the shooting outside continued sporadically, he crawled through the dining room, into the study. Joan Berman was still there unharmed, flattened on the floor by the side window. Mark whispered to her, letting her know what had happened.

'We've got to get out of here!' Joan whispered back fearfully. 'If we don't they'll kill us off one by one!'

'I'm going to check on Anita,' Mark said. 'Don't panic, Joan, you're doing a good job here. I'll get someone else to go on watch in the kitchen, then I'll talk with the other people. Maybe some other approach is called for.'

'Don't keep me wondering all by myself,' Joan whispered. 'Make sure you let me know what's decided.'

'Don't worry, I will,' Mark promised.

The firing outside had completely stopped by the time he crawled out to the parlour. He was gratified to find Anita Walsh still at her post, crouched in a corner with the muzzle-loading Richmond rifle braced at an angle that would cover the front window in case anybody tried to crawl through. He gave Anita the same briefing he had given Joan and told her that maybe it was time to consider some sort of escape plan.

'There hasn't been any more mention of the Green Brigade on the news,' she said. She was using the portable radio with earplug and she unconsciously gave the plug a twist as if it might be nudged into letting her hear better tidings. 'You would think they'd let us know if rescue efforts are underway,' she complained. 'Mark, you tell Charles that if there's a discussion and decisions to be made, I'll vote along with him.'

'Will do,' said Mark.

After the gunfire had ceased for several minutes, Joan Berman forced herself to stick her head up. She did it slowly, holding her breath, clenching the butt of the Union Navy revolver so tightly her fingers hurt. To her great surprise, when her eyes peeped over the sill, a slug didn't crash into her forehead. She had never been so bold in her life, and under such enormous pressure. But she felt she had to make up for her husband. *He* was the one who ought to be up here. Joan resented having to be the hero. She had stuck to her post mainly because she had been too afraid to get up and run, and because of the humiliation she would have felt if both she and her spouse had taken the easy way out.

Through all the bad times in their marriage, Joan had retained a basic respect for Sanford. Till now, she hadn't thought of him as a weakling. She had always been impressed by the drive, determination, and brashness that had made him such a marvellous breadwinner in the tough, intensely competitive insurance business. She had given him all the credit in the world for going to AA on his own and for staying straight up till a few hours ago. But now, under all this stress, something had snapped in her mind, altering her perceptions of him in a fundamental way. Now she dared to consider the notion that maybe she was a better person than he was.

But she had no desire to leave him. Despite all his faults, and maybe because of them, she loved him all the more. She intended to do all in her power to pull them both safely through their present danger. She recognized that she was not doing this out of bravery, but out of primal fear. She was afraid to die, but she was more afraid to go on living without Sanford, whether she lost him to a bullet or to alcoholism.

'You're the only one who hadn't gone on watch yet,' Mark Pearson said to Sanford Berman. 'That's why I'm asking you to go up and cover the kitchen. I'll take another turn in the dining room. That's fair, isn't it?'

'I don't care about fair, I care about smart,' Berman glowered. 'Somebody already died up there, and I'm not dumb enough to be next.'

'If we don't keep them from getting in the house, they'll get us down *here*,' Mark argued. He glanced up the stairs as if to make sure that what he was talking about hadn't already happened; for the time being he had left the trapdoor open to give himself a better chance of hearing if anything went wrong; it could be closed and barred once this argument was settled and the new guards were posted. 'This is our last line of defence, not our first,' he told Sanford.

'I think what happened to Andrea proves what we're doing is hopeless,' interjected Ben Harris. 'I don't want to see my wife go up there again. I'd rather take my chances on some kind of escape attempt.'

'If we can hold out here, the cops are bound to be coming after those terrorists,' said Charles Walsh.

'You just want to protect your precious antiques,' Sanford Berman scoffed. 'Well, the best way to protect them is to get out of here. No one is going to be shooting at the place after we leave. We're the goddamn *target*, for Christ's sake!'

'Even if the cops found the wrecked plane, how do they know which way the Green Brigade went?' said Ben Harris. 'You could lose the population of a small city in these mountains and forests.'

'They'll be using helicopters,' said Mark Pearson.

'Yeah, and they'll have a hundred square miles to search,' Sanford Berman said. 'Even with helicopters they won't be able to see down through the trees. What if they don't get to us in time? I want to go *now*. I have my station wagon parked outside in the courtyard. If these snake people are as brain-damaged as we think, we should be able to outwit them – take them by surprise and drive right through them. Right?'

'I doubt that it would be as easy as you make it sound,' said Charles Walsh.

'Well, I think it's time to try,' said Ben Harris. 'I may be an old man but I have the guts to make a break for it, even if the rest of you don't.'

'I don't think it's a question of guts, but one of intelligent strategy,' Charles pointed out.

'Exactly,' said Mark. 'It's not like we can shoot our way through that freaky mob out there. All we have is Kintay's .45, two Civil War pistols, and a Civil War rifle. Another thing to think about is, assuming the Harrises and the Bermans are going to cut out, there won't be enough of us left at the Manor to even maintain a decent watch to protect ourselves.'

'So come with us,' Ben implored. 'We're not proposing abandoning anybody.'

'What about Kintay?' said Charles.

'Who gives a damn about *him?*' Sanford Berman exclaimed with angry amazement. 'We just leave him, that's all!'

'And George Stone,' Charles added.

'Don't leave my daddy!' Janie cried.

'Don't worry, we won't,' Charles reassured her. 'I was only making the point that your father can't run, and I don't believe we can make it if we carry him. So for me there's no choice but to sit tight.'

'Wait a minute – who *says* we can't carry him?' said Ben Harris. 'George is the one who would be best served if we succeed in getting out of here. He could be taken to a hospital.'

'Look,' said Mark Pearson, facing the Harrises and Sanford Berman. 'We can't keep bullshitting while half the upstairs is without lookouts. Let's make our decisions. Are you people determined to split?'

'If a reasonable plan can be devised,' Sanford hedged, backing down a bit after all his brave bluster. 'You can ask Joan what she's in favour of, but I'm sure she'll tell you I'm the boss.'

'Sophie and I will vote for an escape attempt, too, if it looks plausible,' said Ben Harris.

'All right,' said Mark. He took a deep breath. 'I've got an idea that would be scary to pull off, but if it worked it'd improve all our chances immeasurably. What if a couple of us sneaked outside and took some of the terrorists by surprise – slit their throats commando style? We could grab their guns and ammo. Then those of us who are staying at the Manor would have the means to defend ourselves better, and we could lay down covering fire for the ones taking off in the station wagon.'

'You're crazy!' said Sanford Berman.

'Mark!' Heather gasped, pleadingly grabbing her husband's arm. 'I won't let you go out there to take such a risk!'

The Harrises just stared, utterly flabbergasted by Mark's wild suggestion.

Scarcely believing the sound of his own voice, Charles Walsh heard himself saying, 'I believe I'd be willing to go along with Mark. I don't think his idea is as foolhardy as it sounds. The people out there are slow-thinking and slow-moving. Their strength is in numbers and in firepower. But if we pick on some isolated individuals, we'd stand a good chance.'

'And if you screw up,' said Sanford Berman, '*all* of them are liable to go crazy and wipe us out!'

'I don't think so,' said Mark. 'I think we can select our targets and where we take our shots at them, so if we make a mistake and they go berserk we'll only draw fire on ourselves.' In the flickering lantern glow, he looked Charles Walsh in the eyes. 'I take it you're game to go with me?'

'Yes,' Charles said grimly. He looked at his watch. It was almost midnight. In roughly four hours many of the most important aspects of his life had been wrecked, ruined, desecrated. People close to him had been killed. He knew that he would never get over all of the losses, human and material.

For the moment, because of his grief and fear and sense of outrage, he was becoming a man of action instead of ideas. He was making the transition more easily than he had dreamed possible. It was ironic that, like the creatures threatening him, he was now being driven by the reptile complex. Deep inside his own brain basic, primitive, instinctive urges were taking over – giving him the necessary capacity for aggression and violence to protect and defend himself, his wife, and his territory.

23

Sanford Berman and Ben Harris agreed to take over the lookout posts in the kitchen and dining room while Mark Pearson and Charles Walsh carried out their raid. To get Sanford and Ben to do this, Mark had to persuade them that after all it was in their best interests: if weapons could appropriated from the terrorists the escape attempt would stand a much better chance.

In the basement, Charles and Mark got ready to go out, while Sophie, Heather, and Janie nervously watched. They weren't going to take any guns with them, just knives. Ben and Sanford had insisted on retaining the firearms for use at the lookout posts, saying, 'What if you two guys don't come back? Then we'll be out the weapons and the manpower.' They didn't seem to weigh in the factor that Mark and Charles were taking a heavy risk for the whole group's potential benefit.

The two men already had on dark enough clothing, which they had worn to prevent themselves from being easily spotted at their lookout posts. Now they took the additional precaution of smudging their faces with dirt from the basement floor, first moistening the hard-packed clay to make it pasty enough.

'Ever do anything like this before?' Mark asked.

'This is a first for me,' Charles replied, rubbing dirt into his cheeks. 'I was too young for Korea and too old for Vietnam. In between, I almost got drafted, but graduate school kept me deferred.'

'I'm no expert at hand-to-hand combat either,' Mark admitted. 'I wasn't a Green Beret, but I did have some training in commando tactics at Fort Bragg. I've done some of the stuff in practice but never for real.'

Explaining that a sharp knife alone wouldn't do the trick, because if you cut a man's throat or stabbed him in the heart he might still have a chance to cry out, Mark fashioned a garrote by twisting a loop of picture-hanging wire between two sticks. It was a macabre task, and noticing the dismayed looks on Charles's and Heather's faces, he tried to make light banter. 'I don't suppose there are any secret escape passages in this basement, are there? A hidden tunnel that leads down to the creek? An old mine shaft? I saw a TV movie a while back where an old plantation had a secret tunnel. According to the plot, it had been dug to provide escape from Indians in the early days – but the women and slaves in the story ended up using it to get away from Quantrill and his raiders.'

'A secret tunnel would be lovely,' Charles said wistfully, 'but I'm afraid we don't have one. None that I've come across.' With a twinge of bitter sarcasm, he added, 'If I'd have known we would need one, I'd have had it dug. You see, I was foolish and impractical enough to imagine that the days of battling armed renegades were over, but unfortunately – '

He broke off in mid-sentence because something had occurred to him. Blackening his face with dirt had made him think that soot would have been better, and that had reminded him of –

'The coal chute door. I never took it out when we converted to gas.' He looked at Mark. 'But that wouldn't be any use, would it?'

'I don't know. It may be an alternative way out of here. Where is it?'

'Over here.' Clicking on a flashlight, Charles took Mark to a dark corner behind the gas furnace. He shone the light on the heavy black cast-iron door set into the thick stone, hinged from the top, up close to the rafters.

'Easily big enough for a man to wriggle in and out,' said Mark. 'We can use it, if we oil the hinges. What's outside?'

'Shrubbery. Dense landscaping shrubbery. We didn't want the thing to be an eyesore.'

'Perfect! It'll conceal us. That's how we can sneak in and out to do what we have to do.'

They brought a stepladder over, and Charles fetched an oilcan and a spraycan of DW-40. Mark unbolted the coal chute door and worked carefully on it, applying lubricant liberally and opening it a crack at a time, then swinging it slowly back and forth till the hinges worked almost soundlessly. Upstairs, the doors were barricaded with heavy pieces of furniture; now those cumbersome obstacles wouldn't have to be moved aside. This exit was better suited for stealth and concealment. And it was easy to protect. If Charles and Mark were pursued, they couldn't easily be chased right into the house. Trying to get out and in wouldn't be very dangerous to anyone but themselves.

When they were satisfied with their preparations, Mark went upstairs and crawled from lookout to lookout, letting them know what was going to take place. Then, back downstairs, he gave Heather a meat cleaver and stationed her by the coal chute door. 'Come up the ladder and bolt the door as we leave,' he told her. 'Then wait and listen. Don't leave for a second. When we come back, I'll tap three times softly so you'll know it's us – unless something bad happens, then we might not have time to tap. In that case, we'll be yelling our heads off.'

'Be careful, Mark, I love you,' Heather said, hugging him.

Mark climbed up the ladder first. He opened the door and listened to the night sounds. He couldn't see out very well because of the thick shrubbery. The branches and leaves had spread close to the house, but the roots were a foot or so away. Crawling out, knife in hand, Mark was able to work himself into a sideways position, stretching his body out lengthwise between the stonework and the shrubs. Then Charles did the same thing on the opposite side of the coal chute door. They each wriggled to where they could push aside foliage and peek out into the side yard. They were almost directly beneath the dining room window where Sanford Berman was stationed.

Sanford didn't see them till they started crawling away from the house. At first he jumped and almost bolted – afraid they were a couple of terrorists who could have laid a grenade damn near right under his feet. Then he realized it was Mark and Charles. Under his breath he cursed them for not letting him know that the coal chute door was in that particular spot.

He watched them slowly zigzag towards the shot-up log pile where Janie Stone had been pinned down before her father rescued her. At the moment, the coast was clear for this manoeuvre, but a couple of minutes ago several terrorists had been shuffling about in that area, making Sanford nervous.

Sanford watched Mark and Charles crawl behind the logs. He wondered what the hell they were up to. Sure as shit, he told himself, those two highbrows trying to play hero were going to do something that would cause Sanford Berman to get shot at. Why the hell did they have to be operating on *his* side of the house?

For a long time nothing happened. Sanford kept watching the log pile, working himself into a dither. He thought he had figured out Charles and Mark's plan: they were probably waiting for one or two terrorists to wander close to the pile of logs so they could make their move.

The night breeze wafting through the shot-out windows kept filling Sanford's nostrils with sickening odours. Right in this goddamn dining room happened to be where Brenda and Meredith Meachum had died, and he could smell the sticky-sweet coagulated blood that had soaked into the carpet. Mixed with it was the cloying aroma of the multitudinous brands of wines and liquors that had soaked into the carpet out in the parlour, along with his own vomit. He considered it another item of personal bad luck that the breeze carrying these odours had to be blowing his way. If a goodly volume of rancid urine and faeces could have been mixed in, it would've smelled exactly like the jail in Nashville.

To Sanford's horror, the three terrorists who had been by the log pile earlier, now wandered back into the area. He was beside himself with dread and anticipation. Would the two highbrows be nutty and stupid enough to take on all three? If they did, they'd get killed for sure. All the terrorists would probably flip out and start blasting the house to bits again, or maybe charging it in a suicide assault like the doped-up gooks in Vietnam and Korea. Sanford and Joan and everybody else would get wiped out. Even if by some miracle they survived and still had the heart to make their escape attempt, they'd have to do it without the covering fire that the goddamn highbrows had promised.

The suspense dragged on and on. Sanford was on pins and needles. The three terrorists milled around in front of the log pile like spaced-out robots. Nobody pounced on them. Sanford Berman sweated and clutched the .45 and wondered when the hell he was going to be let off the hook.

Actually, Mark and Charles had been gone from behind the log pile for the past ten minutes. They had used it to screen them as they dropped back into the woods. Then, using the woods for cover, they had worked their way around to the back of the stable.

Mickey Holtz and Janet Fagan were loitering by the corral. An hour ago they had sprayed bullets into the ex-hostage with the spiky orange hair who had killed Andrea

185

Warnak while attempting to rape her. Mickey and Janet had been lovers, with dreams of getting married in a communist ceremony in Havana, Cuba. Now, their brains barely functional, an awareness of what the lewdly naked ex-hostage had been about to do to Andrea began to stimulate their libidos. Gradually their mutual lust overcame their sense of danger, and they sought the shadowy concealment at the side of the stable, where they shed their armaments and equipment and began to peel their clothes off.

From the back of the stable, behind a large oak tree, Mark Pearson and Charles Walsh observed the two terrorists copulating like wild animals, with no preliminary caresses and no displays of affection. They grunted and snorted, rammed and bucked, trying to keep their gasps and cries muffled, not for the sake of decorum, but for fear that the other beasts might be drawn to the scene of their mating. In case this should happen, they kept their weapons near to hand.

Their orgasmic cries were choked off – as Mark Pearson used the garrote on Mickey Holtz, and Charles Walsh yanked Janet Fagan's head back, muffling her mouth with his forearm and slitting her throat with a deep, hard stroke. Holtz took longer to die – he bucked and flailed, but he was lying on his belly with his face shoved into the ground under Mark's weight. 'Help me!' Mark whispered, and Charles plunged his bloody knife into Holtz's back, penetrating the heart.

They dragged the nude bodies of the dead terrorists behind the stable. Then they gathered up two Uzi sub-machine guns and two khaki belts and bandoleers weighted down with grenades, ammo pouches, spare clips, and sheathed bayonets. They ducked back into the woods. Then, retracing their path slowly and trying not to make any disturbing sounds, they skirted the house once again and finally crawled out of the woods, ending up behind the log pile.

Here they took a breather. 'Are you okay?' Mark whispered, fearing that Charles might have been badly shaken by his first act of killing. For his own part, Mark felt surprisingly little emotion except relief that so far things had gone well.

'Yes, I can keep going,' Charles whispered back, figuring that Mark must be worried about his endurance since he was older and presumably more bookish. Like Mark, Charles did not feel guilt or remorse over their escapade. Maybe it was because the terrorists with their damaged brains could be thought of as less than human. They had reminded Charles of dangerous, primordial beasts. Poised to attack them, he had felt the same blood-pounding fear and awe of the beasts and of his own daring as primitive man must have felt when confronting sabre-toothed tigers. Now he felt relief and astonishment – even exhilaration – that he and Mark had got away with it.

Well, not quite. They still had to make the remaining fifty feet to the coal chute door. They peered out from behind the log pile, and the stretch they had to crawl appeared to be clear.

Sanford Berman was watching from the dining room window, and saw Mark and Charles briefly stick their heads out. He wanted to warn them but he was scared to cry out. While they had been gone, three terrorists who had been in the area of the log pile had wandered across the driveway and behind some tall forsythia bushes. They were now out of sight, but they might be close enough to pounce on Mark and Charles.

While the two 'highbrows' had been gone, Sanford had finally figured out what they must be up to – and had been surprised and relieved that they had the good sense not to try to jump any of the terrorists close to the house.

Now that they were back, they must have captured some weapons, so Sanford wanted them to make it to safety for his own selfish reasons.

But how could he warn them? He didn't dare. He wasn't even sure they were in danger. If he yelled to them to watch out, he might get shot.

Mark and Charles sneaked out from behind the log pile – crawling commando style, keeping as low to the ground as possible, and trying to be careful dragging their haul of weapons.

A grenade clattered against a machine-gun barrel.

Three terrorists stepped out from behind the forsythia bushes. One of them unslung a crossbow from his shoulders, loaded, and cocked. The other two aimed automatic rifles at the two crawling men.

Sanford Berman pointed his .45 at the terrorist with the crossbow. Somehow the idea of a bolt loaded with snake venom flying through the air was more hateful and repugnant to him than the thought of guns spitting bullets – and reflexively he got the one with the crossbow in his sights first. But he didn't pull the trigger. Instead he broke out in a cold sweat, scared that if he couldn't get all three, they'd get him. On the other hand, he could fire and duck – and with luck maybe Mark and Charles could use one of their captured guns to finish off the other terrorists. But what if it didn't work? What if Sanford missed? Then what would he have accomplished for risking his neck?

While Sanford was deciding to be a coward, Mark and Charles got half way to the coal chute door. Then there was a loud twang – and a crossbow bolt buried itself in the ground inches from Charles's head. He rolled away from the impact. At the same time, the terrorists with automatic rifles opened fire, squeezing their triggers over and over, and the rifles kept going click . . . click . . . click . . . click. Mark had scrambled behind a tree, in a

188

firing crouch with one of the captured Uzis. When he realized that the two clicking rifles weren't going to hurt him, he drew a bead on the terrorist with the crossbow – who was slinking away in a slow, zombie-like gait. Charles was fumbling with the other Uzi, getting it aimed, trying to find the safety catch.

'Hold your fire, Charles!' Mark whispered. He had decided to let the terrorist with the crossbow get away – it was better than opening fire and risking retaliation from hordes of the automatons.

'What are we going to do?' Charles whispered back. He edged his body sideways so it was partially protected by the tree behind which Mark was crouched.

'Wait!' Mark hissed. 'See what happens!'

'They'll come after us with knives, that's what.'

'I hope they do.'

Click . . . click . . . click . . . click. The two terrorists kept clicking their weapons like children playing with toy guns. Like idiots who will keep trying to insert a square into a star-shaped hole, they didn't try something else. They didn't draw knives. They didn't start swinging their rifles like clubs. Within a couple of minutes – which seemed much longer to Mark and Charles – the short attention span of the brain-damaged creatures came into play . . . and they simply wandered off, slowly, absent-mindedly, slinging their rifles on their backs.

'Well, I'll be damned,' Sanford Berman said under his breath. He began convincing himself that he had not really acted in a cowardly way. He had been right not to do anything. Everything had turned out fine. In fact, comfort could be taken in seeing how slow-moving, stupid, and ineffectual the terrorists were. It ought to bode well for the escape attempt.

Bolstered by this line of reasoning, Sanford kept watch for a while longer, hoping that Mark and Charles would have no more close calls before they crawled through the coal chute with their precious load of weapons.

Mark was angry when he and Charles climbed back down into the basement to find Sanford Berman and Ben Harris already there. 'You two guys are really anxious to desert your posts, aren't you?' You're leaving half the main floor unguarded.'

'Well, we're going to be splitting anyways,' Berman defended brashly. 'I saw you and Charles make it back with the weapons, and I figured we shouldn't waste any more time now. Good job, by the way.' Sandford winked. 'You were never in as much hot water as you probably thought. When that mug with the crossbow stepped out, I had you covered with the .45.'

'Why didn't you shoot him, then?' Mark demanded. 'I suggest you get back upstairs and take a head count on the terrorists. Try to figure out how many you're gonna be up against and where they'll be before you try to break through them.'

'Good idea,' said Ben Harris, trying to ease the dissension.

While Charles and Mark checked over all the weapons, loaded the two Uzis, and made sure the mechanisms were functioning, the four lookouts did a count from each of the four sides of the house. Mark had them make sketches of what they saw, so any overlaps of field-of-view could be taken into account. The tally seemed to be about thirty-one people outside, give or take a few who may have moved and got counted twice.

'According to the news report I saw on TV,' said Charles, 'forty-three Green Brigade members and twelve hostages were on the plane when it left LaGuardia. Subtracting the ones we know are dead, and Kintay, that leaves forty-seven. But we only have a head count of thirty-one. So sixteen more could be lurking just about anywhere, split up or in groups.'

'What are you driving at?' asked Ben Harris.

Charles said, 'When you make your break you'll be going against unknown odds. You may get off this property, only to encounter more danger on the road somewhere.'

'Don't try to scare us into changing our minds and staying!' barked Sanford Berman. 'I have a feeling whoever is stuck in this hole is gonna be done for! The rest of you are welcome to come with us!'

'No, thanks,' said Mark Pearson. 'In about five more hours it'll be daylight. We've made it so far by holding down the fort. We ought to be able to stick it out a few more hours till help comes.'

'*If* it comes,' said Ben Pearson.

'It'll come,' Mark stated confidently.

Charles Walsh didn't bother entering into the argument. He was committed to protecting his own homestead. Maybe Carson Manor was in a shambles, but he still had hopes it could be salvaged – as long as they didn't abandon the place and let the terrorists go wild and raze it to the ground.

Sanford Berman was glad nobody took him up on his offer. He didn't want to lose his covering fire. He pictured a regular fusillade being laid down from the house – but that wasn't what Mark Pearson had in mind.

'We're not going to shoot from the windows and draw more fire on the Manor,' Mark said. 'Charles and I will sneak outside again and take up a position behind the log pile. All you people have to do is get in the station wagon and gun it out. We'll cover you when you peel across the courtyard. Once you're out to the driveway, you're on your own.'

'Shit! You're not giving us enough help!' Berman complained.

'Take it or leave it,' said Mark. 'You're leaving us shorthanded, with a man who can't walk.'

'It'll have to do,' said Ben Harris, patting Berman on the shoulder. 'C'mon . . . let's get started.'

The Harrises, the Bermans, Mark Pearson, and Charles Walsh used the coal chute door to sneak out and crawl, two at a time, to the staging area behind the log pile. All of the seven vehicles owned by George Stone, the Meachums, the Walshes, and the four couples who had shown up for the marriage encounter were parked twenty feet from the opposite side of the driveway, their grilles aligned with the outer curve of the brick courtyard. The Bermans' blue Dodge station wagon was the third vehicle in the line, after George Stone's pickup and the Pearsons' red Camaro.

There were about fifteen terrorists and/or brain-damaged ex-hostages milling about the front lawn. It was hard to get an accurate count because some were in the partial darkness under willow and sycamore trees. As it happened, at this particular moment none were in the area between the log pile and the vehicles.

Charles and Mark took up firing positions behind the logs. Then, as Mark had advised them to do, the Bermans and the Harrises started moving towards the station wagon, refraining from running, which would have immediately drawn attention. Instead they walked slowly in a loosely-knit group, imitating the halting, uncoordinated gait of the brain-damaged ones they were hoping to pass for. All went well till Sanford unlocked the station wagon and opened the door. Soon as the interior light came on, shots rang out. Then all of the escapees screamed and scrambled to get in the car while Sanford dived to pull the locks up.

Terrorists were coming across the lawn, shooting at the station wagon. Mark and Charles opened fire on them.

Sanford got the engine started and in his panic, he put the headlights on. Mark had told him not to, rather to drive by moonlight. Bullets started to zero in on the lit-up vehicle and one headlight was immediately shot out as Sanford jammed the gearshift into 'drive' and screeched out, not bothering to back up and turn around. Instead he lurched forward across a section of lawn, trying to get on to the driveway.

Mark gunned down a terrorist in Sanford's path, and the station wagon ran over the terrorist as he fell. Charles shot two more. Some of the terrorists' fire was directed at the two men behind the log pile, while the station wagon reached the driveway and picked up speed. Keeping their heads as low as possible, Mark and Charles continued to spray bullets.

Sanford Berman screamed and ducked as shots shattered his windshield, killing his wife. Ben and Sophie Harris were sprawled half on the floorboards and half on the back seat, cowering in terror.

Sanford thought he was going to make it. He was almost to the bridge over Carson Creek, when a party of terrorists, led by Colonel Mao, stepped out from behind a clump of trees, firing automatic rifles. Sanford was riddled instantly. The station wagon went out of control, smashing into the bridge rail, exploding and bursting into flames. More bullets slammed into the vehicle, killing Ben and Sophie Harris before they had a chance to burn to death.

The explosion and fire drew the attention of the automatons who had been shooting at Mark and Charles. They lost interest in squeezing their triggers and began to wander away towards the orange, smoky flames, which to them were an awesomely thrilling spectacle.

Other terrorists started shooting at the six remaining parked vehicles out of a desire for vengeance coupled with a wish to keep making beautiful fires like the one down by the bridge. While this fiery destruction was raging, Mark and Charles were able to sneak away and re-enter the basement.

24

After the failure of the escape attempt, Charles and Anita Walsh and Mark and Heather Pearson had to figure out how best to go on defending themselves. The deaths of the Bermans and the Harrises had left them shocked and dispirited. Little Janie Stone did not ask any questions because she feared the exact details of the tragedy; instead she sat in benumbed silence, watching over her father.

Charles examined George Stone, who was still unconscious, still perspiring profusely under a high fever. The blackness and swelling around his wound site had spread and worsened. The purpose of venom wasn't only to kill a snake's prey. Since the snake swallowed its meals whole, bones and all, awesome digestive processes had to be brought into play. Venom was a cocktail of potent enzymes that not only poisoned the prey but immediately went to work tenderizing and digesting the flesh. This potency had to be counteracted by the antivenin before too much damage spread to vital organs and blood vessels.

'Is Daddy going to be okay?' Janie asked tremulously.

'Yes, I believe so,' said Charles. 'He's a big, strong man. If the antivenin wasn't working, he . . . he already wouldn't have made it. I think he'll pull through, but we won't know for sure for at least another twenty-four hours.'

Once again Charles thought to himself how fortunate it had been that the crossbow bolt had struck muscle and bone, which had prevented it from going in deeper. If the venom had been injected directly into a major vein or artery, death would have been virtually instantaneous.

The chambers of the heart would have been clogged and ruptured by the coagulating action of the poison.

Janie Stone continued praying for her father. She also prayed for the souls of her mother and grandmother, and for the soul of Blackie the watchdog, even though dogs weren't supposed to have immortal souls. She hoped that somehow this would turn out not to be true so she could be reunited with her family and her dog eventually in the afterlife. The tragedy and trauma that had struck her made her more dependent on God and on prayer, but it had not brought her closer to her church. She doubted that she could ever again respect the snake-handling ceremony or believe it was ordained by the Almighty.

With stethoscope and blood pressure apparatus, Charles examined General Kintay. To take the blood pressure reading, Charles rolled up the khaki sleeve that bore the snake armband, so he would have an excuse to cover up the disgusting emblem. The terrorist leader was in a coma; large portions of his brain had been destroyed by anoxia and possibly by some blow to the top of his head sustained in the plane crash. When Charles removed the gag from Kintay's mouth, he babbled about fascist pigs, flames of freedom, and greetings of profound love to all oppressed people. Charles could have given him a shot of morphine to keep him quiet instead of replacing the gag, but any depressant drug administered to a man in coma might finish him off. Instead Charles tied the gag loosely, restraining Kintay's babbling, yet his shell could still breathe.

'Why are we bothering to keep him alive?' Mark Pearson wanted to know. 'He's no good to us or to himself.'

'I can't let him die,' Charles replied. 'It's one thing to kill them in self-defence or for reasons of survival, but it would be another thing for me to kill one who's helpless and harmless.'

'The Hippocratic oath and all that,' Mark muttered. 'But I'm not so sure that Kintay's harmless, even in his present condition. In a way, he has even more power . . . like a saint who's been martyred.'

'You may be right,' Charles acknowledged. 'In addition to being the seat of rage and aggression, the reptile complex also governs ritualistic behaviour. That's why the terrorists are acting like robots relentlessly carrying out ingrained responses – like loading and firing their weapons over and over.'

'Firing them at us – because we took their leader away,' said Mark. 'If we gave Kintay back to them, they might leave us alone.'

'I doubt it,' said Charles. 'I'm thinking about the way lizards behave. Once they chose their victims, they develop a fixation. They have to carry out what they started. They won't go away until the victims are destroyed. It's as if they forget the cause for their animosity and it no longer matters. All that matters is the rage and its vindication.'

Heather shuddered, sitting next to Mark on the basement steps. 'Ugh!' she said. 'You make out situation sound hopeless. The beasts will not quit till they kill us.'

'We can still carry out the same survival strategy as before,' said Mark. 'And we'd better hop to it before they get tired watching our cars burn and start crawling in through the windows. The sun'll come up in about three hours. That's not too long to hold out. I still think help will come. We're better armed than before. We have enough people to stand watch at the same four windows, and we can still retreat to the basement as a last resort.'

'You mean leave Janie down here with her father – and with Kintay?' said Heather disapprovingly.

'But with the trapdoor open,' said Mark. 'That way if she has a problem she can call for help. And we can

197

scramble down here and bar the door much quicker if we have to.'

Anita shook her head despairingly. She was thinking about the three A.M. news broadcast, which she had heard while the escape attempt was ending fatally and she was helplessly watching the cars blowing up, from her lookout post by the parlour window. She said, 'I'm sorry, but I'm beginning to think help isn't coming. There was still no mention of it on the radio. They keep repeating the same bulletin, with no additional information.'

'The police never tell everything they know,' said Mark. 'When they have a manhunt on, they don't want the quarry to know exactly what they're thinking and doing.'

'But they don't have to be so guarded in this case,' said Heather. 'They're aware that the terrorists are brain damaged and can't react intelligently. The police ought to be mainly concerned about the welfare of innocent people. We don't really know that they *are*. All we're doing is conjecturing and hoping for the best.'

'I guess I've lost faith,' said Anita. 'I've heard of too many cases where the police made the wrong moves, or no moves at all. I think we should depend on ourselves rather than other people.'

'We've got to believe that help is coming,' Mark insisted. 'If it doesn't, we can't hold out here forever.'

Charles Walsh still hated the thought of abandoning Carson Manor to the mercy of the terrorists. He loved the place too much. Even though it had been terribly damaged, so far the destruction wasn't utterly irreparable. Plaster could be mended. Antique furnishings could be replaced gradually, in spite of the great expense. But if dozens of explosive and incendiary grenades were lobbed in, in the absence of anyone to defend against such action . . .

But Charles didn't want to sacrifice more human lives

198

for his love of his property. He wasn't sure they could continue to defend it. He wasn't sure they could continue to be safe here. He couldn't place a greater value on human life than on real estate, no matter how aesthetically pleasing that real estate was. He would then be no better than the brain-damaged ones with their primitive, bestial compulsion to fight to the death over territory.

'What about someplace else?' said Charles. 'Maybe if we could somehow make it to someplace easier to defend . . .'

'Where?' challenged Mark, dismissing the notion with the incredulity in his voice.

'Just wishful thinking, I guess,' Charles said, deflated. Picking up his Uzi and slinging it over his shoulder, he went on voicing his thoughts in a tired, desperate way. 'The escape attempt . . . there were things about it that worked. I wonder if perhaps a slightly different approach might have been successful. Some kind of infiltration, Mark – the way you and I did when we went out and captured weapons . . .' He broke off, shaking his head. 'But we'd all be on foot . . . and there are more of us who would have to infiltrate through . . . and where would we run to?'

'George Stone can't walk, much less run,' Anita reminded them. 'Even if we did have a place to run to, we'd have to carry him, and we'd never make it.'

'The cave. The cave on top of the cliff,' Janie Stone interjected.

The four adults turned towards the little girl and gave her their full attention.

'You remember the cave, Doctor Chuck . . . Doctor Anita. I took you there two summers ago . . . when we went on a hike and picnic.'

25

Crouching by the log pile, Mark and Charles covered the area with their Uzi submachine guns while Anita, Heather, and Janie crawled towards them, through the coal chute door. Most of the terrorists who had been on that side of the house were now gone, drawn like moths towards the flaming vehicles in the brick courtyard. But just when things appeared to be going too well, a shadowy figure lurched out of the darkness towards Anita, Heather, and Janie. Charles almost fired, but Mark stopped him, tugging his sleeve. Sensing danger, the women froze, lying flat on their stomachs, staring as Mark crept out into the open and clubbed the terrorist over the head with the butt of his Uzi, then caught him as he slumped and eased him to the ground. There was a metallic glint as Mark's bayonet was unsheathed, and a soft gurgle as he slit the unconscious terrorist's throat. Heather shuddered. Then, behind Anita and Janie, she continued crawling towards the log pile.

After some brief hugs when the women got to safety, the men turned over their Uzis and Anita and Heather covered Mark and Charles while they crawled back into the house to bring out George Stone and General Kintay. Stretchers had been fashioned from two webbed aluminium lawn chairs that had been stored in the basement, but there was no way to squeeze the stretchers and their burdens through the narrow, awkward opening of the coal chute. So Mark and Charles had to carry Stone and Kintay out one at a time, through the kitchen. Before attempting it, they had carefully and quietly to move aside the huge refrigerator barricading the kitchen door.

Despite themselves, they couldn't do all this without making considerable noise. From behind the log pile, Anita and Heather and Janie held their breath, alarmed by each creak and groan as the heavy refrigerator was shoved and shimmied. Finally the kitchen door cracked open. Then Mark and Charles came sneaking across the back yard, trotting stoop-shouldered, with George Stone on the first stretcher.

'Leave Kintay!' Heather whispered. 'Don't go back in for him – it's too dangerous.'

'We've got to,' Mark told her. 'We have plans for him, don't forget. He doesn't know it, but he's on our side now.'

Despite the fears of the women, Mark and Charles sneaked back into the house. Luckily, no terrorists got in their way, and they were able to bring Kintay out, on the second stretcher. They took a moment to get their breath. Then they all got going. From the log pile, they dropped back into the woods, Anita and Heather carrying George Stone's stretcher, and Mark and Charles carrying Kintay's. Concealed by foliage, they skirted the clearing where the estate was situated. Then, while the women once again covered them with the Uzis, the two men crawled, dragging the homemade stretcher containing Kintay's inert body, till they were beneath an ancient weeping willow tree that furnished an umbrella of darkness in a spot halfway between the log pile and the bridge where the Berman's station wagon was still smouldering.

'Time to put Kintay to work,' Mark whispered. 'He's going to deliver some special messages for us.'

Charles did not find Mark's macabre joke very funny. The 'messages' he was referring to were going to be lethal. Charles looked on uneasily as Mark set five of them in various places beneath Kintay's body.

'I think they'll get the messages loud and clear,' Mark said.

The two men crept back into the woods, rejoining the women.

They failed to spot the terrorist with the crossbow. His weapon was loaded with another hollowed-out bolt filled with venom. Like a slithering snake, he did not give himself away. He waited till Charles, Mark, Heather, and Anita faded into the deeper foliage, where they thought they were relatively safe. Then he shadowed them, ever so stealthily, till they reached the place where Janie was waiting with her wounded father. From behind a bush, he drew a bead on one of the men.

Twaaannnng!

THOCK!!

The bolt thocked into a tree trunk as Mark bent to pick up his end of the homemade stretcher.

Heather whirled to open fire on the terrorist who was fumbling to load another bolt.

'No! *Don't!*' Charles hissed. Afraid that the sound of bullets would draw more of the automatons, he dashed between trees and leapt over a log – trying quickly and silently to cover the twenty feet between himself and the man who was cocking the crossbow. The brain-damaged terrorist was totally focused on his task, but was slow at it. Charles ploughed into him like a guard hitting a quarterback, doing what he had seen on television, even though he had never played anything but touch football. The crossbow went flying. The automaton grunted, the wind knocked out of him as he smacked the ground with Charles on top of him. Groaning, he weakly tried to lift his arms to protect himself, but Charles drove an elbow into the bridge of the terrorist's nose, breaking it. Then Charles got his fingers around the man's throat and began choking him, figuring that the nose clogging with blood would make the job easier. By that time Mark had found a heavy rock and he thudded it down on to the terrorist's forehead. The man was now perfectly still, his face and head a bloody mess, but Charles kept choking for a while afterwards. 'Come on,' Mark whispered, pulling Charles off. 'Let's get out of here before *more* come.'

Mark and Charles hoisted George Stone on the make-shift stretcher, trying not to jostle him too much and hoping that he wouldn't cry out in his fever, giving them away. Ahead of them went Anita, armed with an Uzi, then Janie, while with the other Uzi, Heather brought up the rear. Not till they worked their way far from the Manor, deep into the woods, did they dare to head for Carson Creek and ford it in the bright moonlight. Once across, they rested, concealed by foliage, for the two men were exhausted from carrying George Stone, who was a big, heavy man, and the women, including Janie, were loaded down with canteens, backpacks, and weapons.

The terrorist with the crossbow was not dead. Mark's blow with the rock had given him a concussion but had not sent lethal splinters of bone into his brain. Charles had not choked him long enough. It was as if the parts of his brain that were still functioning could be sustained on much less oxygen, since major parts of his brain were inert, no longer demanding sustenance. When he regained consciousness, even through his pain he was driven by the reptilian instinct to stalk prey. The impulse was fired now by rage and a lust for revenge. He picked up his crossbow. Then, dripping blood from his nose and head, he shuffled and staggered through the woods, following a trail of footprints and disturbed foliage, and listening for human sounds way up ahead.

The people he was after were afraid to stop and rest for very long. Soon they picked up their burdens and moved on, huffing and plodding and scratching their way up a path that was steep and rocky. Finally they came to the cliff, and they found it necessary to stop and rest once more before beginning the arduous climb.

'This is perfect,' Mark said. 'Nobody can come up that

cliff unless we want them to, and they can't blast us out without using cannons or maybe helicopters – which the terrorists don't have.'

The refuge consisted of a sheer facing of rock about seventy-five feet high, then a shelf and a cave. A narrow, twisting path led up to the cave, on the right side of the cliff, squeezing between huge boulders and burrowing under tunnels of solid limestone. Some of the places were so snug that the stretcher barely made it, even when turned almost sideways at great discomfort and risk to George Stone. By the time all of the people got safely to the top, and got set up to camp there and defend themselves, it was almost dawn.

The terrorist with the crossbow was still tracking them. He had lost their trail and then had picked it up again after wading across Carson Creek.

26

In the grey light of early dawn, four assault helicopters circled above the heavily wooded mountains, then descended to the site where the wingless Boeing 747 was sprawled like a big aluminium cigar tube with a stoved-in nose.

Teams of khaki-uniformed FBI SWAT men deployed with their weapons, then advanced in combat readiness upon the wreckage, in case some of the terrorists might have returned during the night. Jim Spencer was hoping this had happened. He had purposely left the downed plane unguarded, like a trap, on the chance that some of the lizards might scurry back to their hole.

But everything was as it had been left yesterday. This was reported to Jim Spencer and Sam Bernardi by one of the squad leaders, as they stood beneath the slowly whirring blades of the command chopper.

Spencer ordered the squad leaders to fan their men out and start searching the surrounding woods and the right-of-way for signs of where terrorists or hostages might have headed after jumping down from the plane. The SWAT men knew what to look for: drops of dried blood; tatters of clothing; cast-off equipment, apparel, or accessories; footprints; broken-down weeds; even dead or wounded people who hadn't been able to make it too far from the aircraft.

Sam Bernardi had no specifically delineated role in the mop-up, since his official assignment had been to pilot the LearJet, which had been left in a hangar in Charlottesville. Bernardi was pretending for Spencer's benefit that he was gung-ho, anxious to do more than his share, so that Spencer wouldn't order him to stay out of the way. But he had turned down Spencer's offer of a submachine gun and was carrying only a .45.

Spencer was chain-smoking cigarettes. His eyes gleamed with exhaustion, anger, and anticipation. He was armed with both a .45 and a submachine gun. Last night, from Richmond, he had tried phoning his daughter. No answer. Then at four A.M. he had tried again, letting the phone ring twenty times. Still no answer. He wondered what in the hell Caroline was doing. He wondered if he cared anymore.

Bernardi wanted to calm Spencer down. He had seen bloodlust before in men's eyes, in combat. Spencer had already taken a step off the deep end when he had shot the masturbating ex-hostage on the plane. No telling how much farther he would go. He looked just about ready to shoot anything that crossed his path. 'All we have to do is take prisoners,' Bernardi said. 'Round up all the terrorists and hostages. Our story about what went wrong won't be able to be challenged.'

'Unless somehow somebody didn't get brain-damaged enough,' Spencer said in a hard, brittle tone.

'How would that be possible?' Bernardi asked, hoping that Spencer didn't have a logical answer.

'I don't know. Maybe somebody got lucky and found some trapped air. A pocket of oxygen.'

'I really doubt it, Jim,' said Bernardi.

'We'll see,' Spencer told him. 'I don't want to leave any witnesses who can still talk coherently about what happened. The director agrees. I spoke with him last night. He wants the lid shut down tight.'

At Carson Manor, a few of the terrorists had discovered a wondrous thing: General Kintay had appeared among them once more. The rising sun had revealed him, lying flat on his back under a tree. Drawn to their leader, they congregated around his body, which was very still, bound hand and foot. They muttered among themselves, making low, babbling sounds, as more and more of their comrades began to gather around.

Colonel Mao came to the resting place of her lover, and the others moved aside to allow her to approach. She knelt at Kintay's side, wondering if he might be dead. But her addled, fixated brain refused to believe that it could be so.

The others babbled and grunted, waiting for her to do something.

She felt a compulsion to arrange Kintay into a more lifelike and less helpless posture, as if she could recapture the powerful charisma that she dimly remembered.

She reached out to untie his hands, turning him over to do so. She then saw the grenades – the detonating handles popping up – the handles that had been held down by Kintay's weight. She couldn't quite grasp the meaning of the trick that had been played on her, but somehow she sensed there was something to fear.

Then the grenades exploded, ending her struggle to comprehend.

From the cave on the cliff, Dr Charles Walsh heard the exploding grenades and, knowing what it must mean, he was ashamed of himself. He had given Kintay the injection of morphine to keep him quiet and still so his body could be booby-trapped. He had taken a helpless person's life.

'The messages have been delivered,' Mark Pearson said with satisfaction. 'I hope Kintay took plenty of his comrades with him into eternity or wherever communist atheists go. Now there will be fewer of them for us to contend with.'

This was true. But nevertheless Charles felt guilty for going along with Mark's idea of booby-trapping Kintay's unconscious body. He was a physician, and he had taken an oath to minister to the sick and injured, not to kill them when they were unable to defend themselves, no matter what crimes they may have committed while they were healthy.

When the decision had been made to try to escape to the cave on the cliff, Mark had said, 'We can't carry Kintay and George Stone *both* through the woods – we don't have the manpower. So why don't we make Kintay come over to *our* side? I think we can "persuade" him to perform a suicide mission for us.'

Listening to Mark explaining his idea, Charles hadn't been as shocked or as determined to stick to his principles as he ought to have been. With only a token protest, he had capitulated to Mark's argument that 'we may have to fight our way out of the cave, even if we manage to make it there. Help may not come. The terrorists may stalk us – like the lizards you described, who keep coming after their prey no matter what. If we can eliminate some of them now, so much the better.'

Charles had injected the morphine and helped set the deadly trap with a live man as bait, and he wasn't sure whether his truest, deepest motive was self-preservation or revenge. Maybe he had just wanted to make Kintay pay for the destruction of Carson Manor by sentencing him to death without a trial. He was surprised that it had taken Kintay's followers all this time to find his body and carry out the execution. But that had been the plan: to let the shadows obscure the bier till rays of sunlight poked through the branches of the weeping willow tree.

First Charles and the others on the cliff had heard the helicopters off to the west. And after that, the louder, closer sound of the grenades being detonated.

'What happened to the helicopters?' Heather asked. 'How come we don't hear them anymore? Did they go away?' She sounded desperate, afraid to lose the possibility of salvation.

'They must've landed,' Mark said reassuringly. 'I imagine they're checking out the place where the plane went down. They'll start spreading out, combing the area for signs of the terrorists.'

'What if they mistake us for terrorists when they spot us?' said Anita. 'If they spot us. They might not even fly this way.'

'They will sooner or later,' Mark insisted. 'But you're right, we've got to be careful. We don't want to run out waving our guns.'

'A white flag,' said Charles. 'I'll take off my shirt and make a white flag on a stick.'

While they talked and listened for the helicopters to start whirring again, the terrorist with the crossbow found his way to the cliff. He heard the voices up there. He watched from concealment, but he couldn't see the people. From the ground, he did not have a good angle to pick anybody off. Still dripping blood from his nose and head, he skirted the field of view of the people, then stealthily worked his way over to the twisty, rocky path and began to climb it.

When Jim Spencer heard the exploding grenades, he ordered his SWAT commandos to board their choppers and begin an aerial search in the direction where the explosion seemed to have come from. In the command chopper with Sam Bernardi next to him, Spencer studied a map of the heavily wooded countryside below them. On a straight line, Carson Manor was only three miles from the crashed Boeing 747, so it didn't take very long to get there by air.

'There they are!' the helicopter pilot cried out. 'Looks like twenty-five or thirty of them down there, Commander!'

'Makes sense,' Spencer said with satisfaction. 'According to the map, this Carson Manor is just about the only place around that anybody would want to bother with.'

Over the flight-command radio, Spencer ordered the other three choppers to hang back and hover so as not to alarm the terrorists too much, assuming they might be capable of thinking clearly enough to be scared by the presence of assault aircraft, while the command chopper made a slow circle over the grounds of the estate. Spencer and Bernardi saw the burnt-out vehicles, the dead bodies, the slaughtered horses. They took note of the way the shot-up mansion was surrounded by automatons, some armed and some unarmed. A few of them glanced up at the helicopter as it made its slow pass over their heads, but most of them did not waver from watching the house, as if they were fixated by it.

'Looks like somebody's holding them off pretty well!' said Sam Bernardi.

Spencer ignored the comment. Bernardi got the idea that Spencer would rather not find the owners of the mansion still alive. That way there would be no one to dispute the official FBI account of the mop-up.

Over the flight-command radio, Spencer ordered the other three helicopters to take positions at the three corners of the estate not covered by the command helicopter. Thus the attack zone was split into four quadrants. The four helicopters didn't land right away. Instead, on a signal from Spencer, they simultaneously closed in to hover and strafe, each craft concentrating fire in its particular quadrant.

Some of the Green Brigade tried to fight back, but their dull, inept reactions were no match for the hovering, methodical spray of bullets from mounted machine guns. The choppers kept circling and strafing, cutting their human targets to ribbons.

From the air, the chopper crews could not distinguish

between terrorists and ex-hostages. They just kept pressing their machine gun buttons.

Sam Bernardi was repulsed and sickened by the carnage, which to him was immoral and unnecessary. He had tagged along on the mop-up, envisioning most of it taking place on the ground, where he might have been instrumental in saving lives. But up here in the air he was helpless. No discretion was being used in selecting targets. He felt the same outraged futility he had felt in Vietnam when he had seen innocent women and children gunned down. He didn't see any reason why prisoners couldn't have been taken. Canisters of tear gas could have been dropped to help neutralize the terrorists, then they and their former hostages could have been rounded up fairly easily. But Jim Spencer apparently didn't want to bother.

When three ex-hostages ran into the stable, Spencer ordered it destroyed by incendiary bombs. The same fate befell two uniformed Green Brigade members who tried to hide in the old cook house. The buildings reduced to flames and rubble, a couple of the brain-damaged ones staggered out, their skin and clothing on fire, and were immediately machine-gunned to death.

Despite being hemmed in by such a murderous barrage, about a dozen terrorists and/or ex-hostages managed to make it into the woods. Spencer ordered the helicopters to land so the SWAT commandos could deploy and pursue.

As the choppers descended with their whirring blades, two figures – possibly unarmed – darted from behind the log pile as if the chopper noise coming so close may have frightened them more than the bullets. They scurried up the steps of the back porch and in through the kitchen door, and nobody happened to be in a position to get a good shot at them. Spencer let a squad of men go after the ones who had dashed into the woods, while with the thirty remaining men he surrounded the house, which seemed eerily quiet and still.

'Come on out of there!' Spencer barked. 'This is the FBI! Drop your weapons and come out with your hands up!'

Sam Bernardi noticed the way Jim Spencer was clutching his submachine gun. 'Jim,' Bernardi cautioned, 'we don't know who else may be in the house. Innocent people may still be alive in there.'

Spencer yelled again. 'This is the FBI! Drop your weapons and come out with your hands up!'

There was no reply. All was deathly silence.

'Let me take a couple of men and go in,' Bernardi pleaded. 'Leave it to me, Jim. I promise you we'll bring out a couple of dead terrorists.'

'There may be more than a couple,' Spencer replied grimly.

From back in the woods there were staccato bursts of gunfire. The SWAT men must have caught up with some of the brain-damaged ones. The barking of their weapons seemed to inflame Spencer. 'I'm going to demolish the place,' he said through clenched teeth. 'It's too dangerous to go in and root them out. We can just open fire with everything we've got and blow it all to hell.'

'What if there are innocent people in there?' said Bernardi. 'Somebody might be wounded, unconscious, or under the gun and scared to call for help.'

'I yelled at them to come out,' said Spencer. 'I gave them a chance. In fact I gave them two chances.'

Bernardi, who was haunted by memories of women and children incinerated in grass huts in Vietnam and Laos, could see that Spencer was only too anxious to bombard Carson Manor with machine guns, grenade launchers, and incendiary mortar shells. Nobody inside would survive such a holocaust. Nothing would be left of the Manor but rubble and flames, blackening the sky.

'Tear gas,' Bernardi suggested to Spencer. 'Why don't we try tear gas? If it doesn't work, then you can use your firepower.'

Spencer looked at Bernardi and almost smiled. There was an unmistakably wry gleam in his eyes, as if he were amused by Bernardi's squeamishness. 'All right,' he said, 'let's give it a whirl. Let's try fumigating the cockroaches.'

He ordered a squad of men with grenade launchers to shoot tear gas canisters through the windows. The missiles smashed through shattered glass, popping and hissing as the stinging gas was released. Then, suddenly, there were some stumbling sounds from inside the house, followed by horrid coughing and retching.

The men surrounding the mansion aimed their weapons at the exit points. Halfheartedly clutching his .45, Bernardi glanced at Spencer. The FBI commander's eyes were narrow slits. He was staring fixedly at the kitchen doorway, his finger tightening on the trigger of his sub-machine gun.

From inside the house came some agonized screaming. A wooden chair came hurtling through a back window – followed closely by a human body that plummeted to the grass. It was a middle-aged man in street clothes, his face and forearms lacerated, bleeding all over his shortsleeved white shirt. He got up, coughing and groping, blinded by tear gas. At that same moment, a young woman staggered out of the kitchen and fell against the railing of the back porch. She was groaning. Her blouse was streaked with vomit.

'Wait!' Bernardi yelled.

But Jim Spencer opened fire. The man and the woman were hammered back and lifted off of their feet by the force of the .30 calibre submachine gun bullets.

'Christ!' Bernardi cried out, staring at the riddled, bloody corpses. 'Christ, Spencer! You didn't even try to make sure who you were shooting at!'

Up on the cliff, outside the mouth of the cave, the survivors of Carson Manor listened to the FBI gunfire, which to them was the sound of salvation.

Janie Stone cowered and trembled against Anita Walsh. 'You don't have to be afraid anymore, honey,' Anita told the child. 'Hear that? It means people are coming to rescue us. We'll soon be able to get your father to a hospital.'

Covered with a blanket, George Stone was sleeping leadenly, dreaming morphine dreams because of the injection Anita had just given him to ease the pain of the tissue-destroying venom.

Charles Walsh peered through his binoculars to scan the horizon in the direction of Carson Manor, but because of the dense forest he couldn't see any of the activity on the grounds of the estate. All he could see was thick black smoke rising above the treetops. He hoped this didn't mean what he feared. But he tried to begin accepting the possibility that the Manor may have been destroyed. He told himself that the loss of the property was not as important as the lives that had been saved.

Mark and Heather Pearson were keeping watch from behind a boulder, at the top of the rocky path that led up to the cliff. Mark put his arm protectively around Heather's shoulders, and they gazed at each other wearily and hopefully, but they did not relax their vigilance with the Uzi submachine guns.

The terrorist with the crossbow, unknown to them, was still silently and slowly creeping up the winding path.

Spencer smiled over the barrel of his smoking gun. It was a bizarre smile, edged with contempt and perhaps with madness. He said to Bernardi, 'I couldn't help noticing you weren't shooting, Sam. What's the matter? Don't you approve of my tactics?'

'Hardly,' Bernardi admitted, his voice dry and husky

214

with defiance – an open defiance of senseless slaughter that had gone unexpressed for years.

'Either you're with me or against me,' Spencer said coldly. 'Just because you volunteered for this, it doesn't mean you can hold yourself aloof from the dirty work. I don't want your .45 to be the only weapon not fired, like you're a dissenter or something. We're all in this together, all taking a fair share of the responsibility. Understand, Sam?'

Bernardi nodded, gulping back stomach acid that had risen into his throat. He realized that if he openly disobeyed one of Spencer's orders, he might not come out of this alive. In fact it probably wasn't beyond Spencer to shoot him in the back and claim he had died in the line of duty.

Again Spencer flashed his strange smile. Bernardi swore to himself that he had seen that same half-vacant look before, on the faces of commanders who no longer cared about anything but body count. 'Come with me, Sam,' Spencer said with an odd cheerfulness. 'All the action isn't over yet. There's still an opportunity for you to hold up your end of the mission. Remember, whatever we have to do here, it's not our fault. The Green Brigade set all this in motion. They're to blame for the slaughter.'

Bernardi forced himself to follow Spencer towards the section of woods where a dozen or so brain-damaged people had recently fled. On the way, Spencer stopped a man carrying a walkie-talkie and told him to relay orders to two of the SWAT squads to board their helicopters and start fanning out, continuing the aerial search of the countryside. He also ordered a third SWAT squad to return to the site where the 747 was down and keep a guard around it.

Meanwhile the leader of the fourth squad came out of the woods and reported to Spencer. 'I think we got them all, Commander. Fourteen of them, some armed and some unarmed. My men are dragging the bodies out now. However . . .'

'However what?'

'We found some signs of a struggle that must've taken place several hours ago. Dried blood on the ground. A crossbow bolt stuck in a tree. Looks like somebody was wounded but didn't stay down. I don't know that it's worth sending a whole squad after him. He must have a helluva lead on us by now. If he comes out into the open, maybe he can be spotted more easily from a chopper.'

'Somebody had to check it out,' said Spencer. 'Even if he died in the woods, we've gotta know for sure.' He turned towards Bernardi, eyeing him piercingly. 'Right, Sam?'

Bernardi refrained from answering. Spencer chuckled as if they were both enjoying a private joke.

'Commander, what do you want me to do?' asked the squad leader.

'Give me a walkie-talkie. Sam and I are going to track those bloodstains. You and your men finish with the body count here, then keep this area secure. We don't want any civilians or local cops poking their noses around.'

The people on the cliff could hear whirring chopper blades way off, in several directions. They watched the brightening sky with increasing hopefulness, but none of the helicopters came their way.

'It's only a matter of time,' said Mark to Heather. 'I'm sure they're carrying out a systematic search. When they get finished working one area, they'll move to another. Eventually they'll find us.'

Charles Walsh hugged Anita and Janie. 'We're all right now,' he said confidently. 'Everything is going to be fine.' In his right hand he clutched the flag on a stick that he had made by ripping up his white shirt. Soon as one of

216

those choppers came into sight, he intended to start waving it like mad.

The terrorist with the crossbow was almost halfway up the path now. It was a steep, difficult climb, and he could barely get enough breath because the blood from his broken nose was caked in his nostrils and septum. He didn't have much of a mind left. But instinctively he appreciated the need for slyness and stealth. His progress towards his prey was very, very slow.

Starting from the place where the squad leader had shown them the crossbow bolt embedded in a tree and the rock caked with dried blood, Jim Spencer and Sam Bernardi had tracked their quarry through the forest to the banks of Carson Creek. Then they had forded the creek to pick up the trail on the other side.

Now they could tell that they were actually following more than one person because the people who had waded across the creek before them hadn't bothered to remove their shoes and boots, and the footprints showed a wide variation in tread pattern. The soaked footgear had left good tracks in several spots – sole patterns in soft dirt, then muddy patterns on rocks that had been stepped upon afterwards. The dried bloodstains didn't always conform to the exact route taken by the majority of the footprints. Therefore it seemed logical that 'the bleeder' had been following the others, tracking them and sometimes losing their trail, then having to pick it up again.

'Five or six people, that's what I figure,' said Spencer.

'They could be people from the Manor,' said Bernardi. 'If so, somebody could be after them. Maybe one of the terrorists.'

'The one with the crossbow, I hope,' said Spencer.

Bernardi wondered exactly what Spencer meant. Was he anxious to kill the one with the crossbow, or was he hoping that the killer with the crossbow would catch up to the people first?

Suddenly they heard a helicopter approaching and hovering almost directly over their heads, but they could barely see it because of the dense canopy of foliage. Spencer used his walkie-talkie to contact the pilot and asked what was going on.

'A white flag,' the squawk-box said. 'We've spotted somebody waving a white flag on a shelf of rock to the west.'

'Hang back and hover,' Spencer ordered. 'Don't make any move till I tell you. Sam and I are right under you, on the ground. We're going to check it out.'

Bernardi and Spencer worked their way to the fringes of the little clearing at the foot of the cliff. They peered from behind ground cover and spotted the white flag waving frantically, trying to communicate with the helicopter that wasn't responding.

'You up there! Who are you?' Spencer called out.

The white flag was immediately pulled in, out of sight. There was no verbal response.

'This is the FBI!' Spencer shouted. 'Who are you?'

This time an answer came down from the cliff. 'Charles Walsh, from Carson Manor, with my wife and some friends! Don't shoot! We're not terrorists!'

'Perfect,' Jim Spencer murmured under his breath to Sam Bernardi. Then, into his walkie-talkie, he said, 'Commander One to Chopper Three. We have the situation under control here. Go back to Carson Manor and await further orders.'

The helicopter turned around and flew off to the east, disappearing behind some treetops. The people on the cliff watched it going away, and wondered why.

'Why did you send the chopper away?' Bernardi asked Spencer. 'What if we need it to get those people down?'

'We won't need the helicopter, Sam,' Spencer said.

'We're going to handle this on our own, without any witnesses.'

'What do you mean?' Bernardi blurted. But he was pretty sure he already knew, and the thought made him sick.

'Mr Walsh!' Spencer commanded. 'You and your friends – throw down your weapons! Come out where I can see you, with your hands up!'

'I tell you, we're not terrorists!' Charles Walsh cried in desperate frustration. 'We have a sick man up here! I'd like to get him to a hospital!'

'I believe you!' Spencer shouted. 'This is merely a precaution! Standard operating procedure! You must surrender your weapons before I can help you!'

After a long pause, two Uzi submachine guns, some bayonets, some grenades and bandoleers, were tossed over the edge of the cliff and fell to the ground. But it seemed that the people up there must still be suspicious, for they were remaining back in the mouth of the cave so that they were out of any line of fire from the ground.

'Now come out with your hands up!' Spencer yelled. Then, aiming his submachine gun at the mouth of the cave, he whispered to Sam Bernardi, 'They'll never know what hit them. It'll be over quickly for them. It's the best way.'

'I won't do it!' Bernardi rasped.

'Don't be a fool, Sam,' said Spencer. 'Those people are quite possibly the last living witnesses to any part of this mop-up operation. I told you that the director wants the lid on tight, and it's up to you to help me carry out his wishes.'

'I'm not going to murder civilians!' Bernardi snapped. He cupped his hands around his mouth and started shouting up towards the cave. 'Stay back! Don't come out or you'll be shot! There's a madman down – '

Spencer whirled, swinging the barrel of his submachine

gun at Bernardi. Bernardi tried to bring his .45 into play, but Spencer smacked it out of his hand. Snarling dementedly, the FBI commander said, 'So this is how you want it, Sam? All right, I'll oblige you. You're going to die like a traitor.' His finger tightened on his trigger.

Twaaannnggg!

The crossbow bolt slammed into Spencer's chest, driving him back. He dropped his submachine gun as Bernardi dived for his .45. Sam would have shot Spencer again, but it was unnecessary. The steel bolt had squarely penetrated the heart. The venom in the shaft was superfluous – even without it, the FBI commander would have died instantly. He was dead before he hit the ground.

Bernardi leapt over the corpse and ran across the clearing, taking cover behind one of the boulders that stood at the mouth of the rocky path that snaked up the side of the cliff. He had spotted the terrorist with the crossbow for only an instant – a head ducking down as the bolt went flying. He didn't relish the thought of trying to make it up that steep, narrow path to battle a crossbow with a .45 – and he was trying to steel himself to do it when a terrific explosion rocked him backwards and sent him sprawling on the ground. He crawled around feebly, groggily groping for his footing, hoping that he, too, wasn't about to be struck by a poisonous crossbow bolt.

'Hey, I got him!' Mark Pearson cried. 'I got him with a grenade!'

'Well, I'll be damned,' Bernardi muttered, realizing through his pain and dizziness that at least one of the people on the cliff hadn't been fool enough to surrender every last weapon to Jim Spencer.

Mark and Heather scrambled down the cliff, snatched up the Uzis they had dropped, and used them to cover Bernardi. He was unarmed; his .45 automatic had flown out of his hand when the grenade went off. His ears still ringing, he slumped against a boulder, too stunned to care about keeping his hands above his head.

'Start talking, mister!' Mark snapped. 'Give us a good reason why we shouldn't shoot you!'

Bernardi shook his head slowly, trying to clear the cobwebs. 'I'm the one who tried to warn you,' he said. 'The man who would've shot you is dead. We've gotta get out of here fast. There are others who might think the way he did.'

'We won't get too far on foot,' Mark said, beginning to believe Bernardi. 'We've got a man who's real sick from snake poison.'

'Maybe there's a way,' said Bernardi. 'I'm not thinking too clearly . . . I think it'll work . . . but you've gotta trust me.'

Mark glanced at Heather. She nodded. 'Okay, talk, man,' Mark said.

They listened carefully to Bernardi's plan before they relaxed enough to let him go for Spencer's walkie-talkie. He used it to call for a helicopter. 'Jim Spencer is badly wounded,' Bernardi lied. 'I'm scared he won't pull through – he's got to be airlifted to a hospital. I just need a pilot and a medic. Commander Spencer wants the rest of the men to stay at Carson Manor and keep the area secure.'

When the helicopter landed, Bernardi led the pilot and medic towards Spencer's corpse. 'What the hell's going on?' the medic blurted as soon as he saw that the man they had come to evacuate was beyond help.

'*Freeze!*' Mark Pearson barked, stepping out from behind a tree. He and Heather kept their guns trained on the pilot and medic while Bernardi disarmed them and got them tied and gagged.

When the helicopter took off again, Sam Bernardi was at the controls. On board were George and Janie Stone, Mark and Heather Pearson, Charles and Anita Walsh. By saving them, Bernardi hoped he might partially redeem himself. He might buy some absolution for past evils he had been too weak to prevent. He was going to do his best to get them to Richmond. They were all afraid that at any moment they might be shot out of the sky. They had to make it to a newspaper office or a TV station. They wouldn't be truly safe till they broke their story. Then the people trying to cover it up would be subdued; in the limelight of publicity surrounding the affair, they probably wouldn't dare to exact any sort of revenge. The world would learn how 'the reptile complex' had been unleashed.

Mark and Heather held hands as they continued to scan the sky, hoping not to see any hostile aircraft. 'We're going to make it, babe,' he whispered. She gave his hand a squeeze. She knew he meant that they were going to make it not just through this particular day of danger but together they were going to make their marriage work.

Sitting in the bay of the helicopter, Janie Stone looked down at her father, who was resting comfortably on a stretcher bolted to the fuselage. He wasn't perspiring so much now. His face seemed more placid, more at peace. She said a prayer of thanks. She believed that he was really going to pull through. Maybe the antivenin alone wouldn't have saved him. Maybe the grace of God had helped, too. Maybe the religion taught to her by her mother and grandmother had its grain of truth.

Charles hugged Anita as they kept watch skywards, by a side window of the chopper. 'We must go back,' he told his wife. 'When this is over, we mustn't let Carson Manor crumble and die. George and Janie can stay on and help us rebuild. We've *got* to. We can't let the ones who did this win. We can't let them murder the past.'

Seeing the glint of anger and determination in his tired eyes, Anita told him she knew he was right, and she promised to stick by him, no matter what he wanted to do. She only hoped she would find the strength. Even if they made it home, she knew the struggle wouldn't be over. In the months ahead, she and Charles wouldn't have a stitch of privacy. They'd be swarmed over by reporters, lawyers, insurance investigators, assorted bureaucrats, and government agents. For the rest of their lives they'd probably feel threatened by unseen enemies. They'd always wonder if the FBI or the CIA had an eye on them.

Charles took a deep breath, as if he were already embarking on a tough mission into the future. Even though he had vowed to rebuild Carson Manor, he knew he could never recapture the aura of nostalgia that had once charmed him. Within him, certain sentiments had died. He couldn't resuscitate the genteel fantasies he had once built out of what he liked best from the history books and from his interpretation of the past.

But despite his regrets, he now had a new kind of pride in himself. His ordeal had taught him that when the chips were down the man of ideas could be a man of action. He had been courageous in a terrible crisis, the likes of which most modern men were never called upon to withstand. He had endured sad, heavy losses. Through it all, he had found qualities within himself that he had never been sure he possessed – qualities he had admired in the eighteenth- and nineteenth-century people whose lives he had studied so zealously. They had fought savage Indians and had not given up when their loved ones were killed, their homesteads sacked and burned. Now he had fought modern savages. And he wasn't giving up either. He was going back to claim what was his, and to start over.